T0067879

LEMOY AND HIS DARK RETURN

J. A. ROBINSON

Archway Publishing books may be ordered through booksellers or by contacting:

Archway Publishing
1663 Liberty Drive
Bloomington, IN 47403
www.archwaypublishing.com
844-669-3957

ISBN: 978-1-6657-4664-9 (sc)
ISBN: 978-1-6657-4665-6 (e)

Library of Congress Control Number: 2023912930

Print information available on the last page.

Archway Publishing rev. date: 07/19/2023

To my children,

Kait, Isaiah, Melody, Ashlyn, and Malachi

October 31, 1899

I sense that this is my final journal entry. I am not human anymore. The reflection I see staring back at me is unrecognizable. My master's hands scarred my body. His blood now runs through my veins. I cannot return to my family and the home I once knew; they are unsafe because of what I have become. My will is not my own. The voice inside my head shapes my every thought, and I must obey it.

The covenant I made cannot be broken. What I have become cannot be undone. I long to hear someone say my name so I may remember who I was before so my master will be free. I see how it is written, but I cannot voice it. It has been taken from my mouth; it has faded from my memory. I will now be called by another name. I will be he who is unseen, he whose name is unwritten. I will take my master's place as the ruler of the air and assemble my legion. I will become a god!

CHAPTER 1

THE CHILDREN

Surrounded by darkness, Melinie cried out for help, but no one was coming to rescue her. A dark figure tormented her thoughts with images of death while she dreamed. "Wake up, Melinie!" a voice said.

Melinie was jolted awake. Gasping for air, she tried to open her eyes, but something pressed against them. Her nostrils were clogged up, restricting her breathing.

What's that smell? she wondered. Trying her best to stay calm, she worked to move her arms and legs; they moved a little, but something restricted her movement.

Where am I? She felt extremely claustrophobic, and her anxiety kicked into overdrive. *I have to get out!*

Melinie tried to scream. That was a mistake. She inhaled something deep into her throat; it blocked her airway and caused her to choke. Immediately closing her mouth, she tried swallowing and clearing her throat repeatedly to force whatever it was down so she could breathe.

Nearing the point of passing out from a lack of oxygen, she finally got the lodged mass to descend her throat. After a hard, painful swallow, she could breathe but barely. Now she could taste dirt.

Where am I?

Struggling to breathe and with that taste in her mouth, she realized that dirt surrounded her. *Oh my God!* Flooded with fear, she began to remember what had happened to her. *That thing grabbed me!*

1

The last thing she remembered was a sharp pain in her shoulder and the sensation of being lifted into the air. *Where did it take me? Where am I? I must get out!* Melinie's thoughts triggered emotions she didn't know she had. *Did it bury me?* If she was surrounded by dirt, she must be underground. Since she couldn't see, she was completely disoriented.

Trusting her gut, she frantically began climbing upward. Trying to control her breathing, she took quick, shallow breaths to reduce the amount of dirt entering her mouth.

The lack of oxygen caused fatigue to settle in quickly, making it difficult for her to move. Her lungs burned with every breath. She struggled to keep conscious.

Don't stop, she told herself. But her body began shutting down. The diminished supply of oxygenated blood to her lungs and muscles had taken its toll. She tried to keep climbing, but she was running out of breath and could feel herself slipping away.

"Melinie!" a voice shouted.

Barely conscious, she heard the voice but couldn't respond.

"Mel!" the voice yelled again.

This time Melinie found a way to bring herself back to consciousness. *I know that voice!* she thought. *That's my brother Caleb!*

Fighting to stay awake, Melinie started taking controlled, shallow breaths. The task was challenging since each breath she took caused her lungs to hurt. Knowing Caleb was above her, she forced her body to move, clawing through the deep earth to reach her brother.

Going in and out of consciousness, Melinie fought hard to keep climbing. Her fingers hurt so badly, and she could feel her nails pulling away from the skin. Her shoulders ached severely from where the creature had dug its claws into them as it carried her away.

Don't think about it. Keep climbing! She had to be getting closer; Caleb's voice was getting louder.

Will they find me? she thought. She gasped for air, hoping to get enough strength to keep fighting. *Please,* help me!

Melinie's thoughts vanished along with her strength, and everything went dark.

"Keep looking," Caleb shouted.

"I don't see her anywhere!" Rachelle called. When Melinie had started screaming, her older brother, Caleb, and younger sister, Rachelle, had been downstairs. They had run to her room, and what they had seen there would haunt them for the rest of their lives. A large, shadowy figure with the body of a man but wings like a bat and long, sharp talons snatched up their sister and flew out the window with her.

They ran to the window, but it was too late. Without hesitation, they dashed downstairs to the front door to see whether they could follow the flying figure, but it had already escaped their view.

Filled with adrenaline, Caleb ran to the basement and grabbed a couple of flashlights. He came back and handed one to Rachelle. "Let's go." They headed down the driveway and into the woods, their flashlights lighting the way.

"Which way do we go?" Rachelle asked. "We didn't see where it went; she could be anywhere!"

Frustrated and scared, Caleb yelled, "I don't know!"

They both began to cry, their bodies shaking with fear. Feeling completely hopeless, they sat down, weeping loudly and fearing they had lost their sister.

Caleb looked up through his tears. He noticed something glowing on one of the trees about a hundred yards away. "Look, Rachelle! What is that?"

Rachelle looked up. "Where are you talking about?"

Caleb pointed toward the woods. "There, that bright spot on the tree. Do you see it?"

"Yes! Oh my God, it looks like a red eye," Rachelle exclaimed.

Caleb ran toward the tree, and Rachelle ran after him, not wanting to be left alone.

As they grew closer, the mysterious red glow faded away. Caleb stopped in his tracks. "It's gone! Do you see it anywhere, Rachelle?"

"No, I don't!" Rachelle yelled back. "What *was* that light, Caleb?"

"I don't know, but it's gone now."

"Wait," Rachelle said. "Look! There it is again."

Once again, the large red light, which Rachelle was convinced looked like an eye, started glowing on another tree farther in the woods. "What do we do?" she said.

"I guess we follow it."

Scared to death but determined to find Melinie, Rachelle agreed to follow the light. It appeared to have a pattern. The odd light would shine on a particular tree, then disappear as they got closer, only to appear again on another tree deeper in the woods. They continued to follow it, hoping it would lead them to their sister.

"Do you see her anywhere, Rachelle?"

"No, nowhere!" Rachelle yelled as she struggled not to freak out.

"Just start digging!" yelled Caleb.

"Dig? For what?"

"This dirt looks fresh like it was just put here."

"You think she's under the ground?" Rachelle shrieked.

"Maybe, it took her somewhere! We need to check!"

"OK, Caleb!"

They began to dig feverishly with their hands, hoping their efforts weren't in vain. Fingers bleeding, vision blurred from their tears, they kept digging.

"Caleb!" screamed Rachelle. "Help me!"

He ran to his sister quickly.

"Look!" she cried.

He looked down in the hole she had dug; there was a hand. "It's Mel's!"

Rachelle grabbed Mel's hand while Caleb dug around it. Together they eventually dug Melinie's body out of the ground, pulling her up and laying her on her back.

"Mel!" Caleb yelled.

There was no answer.

"Her hands are ice cold!" Rachelle said, taking one of Mel's hands in hers.

"Go get some water and a blanket, Rachelle! I'm going to start CPR!"

Rachelle ran back toward the house while Caleb began CPR.

"Two breaths and thirty compressions," he said aloud as he worked on bringing her back. "Come on! Wake up, please! Two breaths and thirty compressions." He continued CPR, determined not to give up on her.

Suddenly Mel took a deep breath, followed by several coughs. He helped her to sit upright as she continued to cough. "Mel, it's me, Caleb."

She tried to open her eyes, but they were compacted with dirt. He grabbed his shirt and lightly wiped her eyes so she could see. Ever so slowly, she opened her eyes.

"Caleb, you found me!" Melinie said.

"I'm here, sis!"

She smiled slightly before collapsing from fatigue. Caleb checked her breathing; she was OK.

Rachelle returned with water and a blanket, which they wrapped around her. Wanting to get her home as soon as possible, Caleb carefully lifted her onto his shoulders, and they made their way back to the house.

Their family had just moved to their new home in the country—or it was new to everyone but their dad, since it was the house where he had been raised. When he was a child, his parents had moved to this remote, little town to experience a simpler and safer life away from the big city and its growing crime.

Their dad was very fond of this little town. He told them stories about it so often that they could recite the entire history. They knew the names of each of his childhood friends, including who did what, where it happened, and so on. He built the place up so much in their minds that when he finally let them know about the move, they all felt excited—until they discovered that this little town was so remote that modern technology hadn't yet caught up.

Their dad knew it would be a huge culture shock at first, but after a while, they would learn to love it, just like he did. He figured they spent too much time on their phones and tablets and needed to experience life outside them.

This rural Missouri town didn't have cell towers or fiber optic internet/cable lines. The community petitioned to keep life simple, and somehow, they kept the technology companies at bay for now. The only option was satellite Wi-Fi service from the next town over. Very few residents used it because it provided spotty service at best. Not wanting to leave technology altogether, their dad planned to get it set up but hadn't yet scheduled the technician's appointment. "They'll survive the weekend without it," their dad said.

The family arrived at the house late on a Thursday night. The movers arrived a week earlier, so their personal belongings were there but still boxed up. "That leaves us with plenty to do without getting bored," their dad said.

Before the move, their parents had decided they deserved a weekend away, since they had worked so hard over the last month to get everything packed.

Convincing their oldest daughter, Beth, to watch the kids for the weekend, they gave them all instructions on what needed to be done while they were gone and then left for their trip the following morning.

Beth was twenty-one and didn't live at home anymore. If she had, she would've moved out before moving to the country; she was a city girl through and through. She loved having everything close to her. She was very social and would never give up the friends she had made "to live like the Amish," she had once said.

After dinner, Beth ensured that her siblings did what she had instructed. She grabbed her little brother, Chase, and headed to the grocery store. Unfortunately, while she was gone, Melinie was taken from her room. Being gone and having no cell phone service, Beth was unaware that anything was wrong. That meant her siblings were alone with no one to call or help.

OK, do I buy what Mom put on the grocery list or just wing it? thought Beth. *Eh, I'll just wing it.* She crinkled up the list and tossed it in the trash.

Beth had agreed to watch her siblings and now wondered why she had agreed to do such a crazy thing. *Oh well, I'm sure hanging with them for a weekend will be fun. Besides, I've been missing my little brother.* She hadn't seen him in a bit and wanted some one-on-one time with him anyway.

"Grab a candy bar, Chase, but don't tell Mom!" Beth giggled.

"I won't. Thank you, sissy!"

"You're welcome!" While she was standing in line to check out, a headline on the front page of the local newspaper caught her attention. "Are you serious?"

"What, sissy?"

"Oh, nothing Chase. Just figure out what candy bar you'll get."

"OK!"

The headline said, "Four residents go missing this month."

"Well, that's creepy!" she said.

"What's creepy?" Chase asked.

"You are!" She tickled his belly, and he laughed. *How can four people in a little town like this one just go missing?* she wondered. "Stay close to me, bubby, OK?"

"I will!"

The article disturbed Beth, but she remained silent.

After getting all the supplies loaded in the car, none of which were on the list, she fastened her little brother into his booster seat. As she closed the door, she was startled by what sounded like someone screaming in the distance, having no idea that it was her sister being carried away by a mysterious creature.

With the newspaper headline fresh in her mind, she paused a moment longer to listen for the scream again before getting into the car to drive away. Not hearing the scream again, she figured the sound must have been some kids playing. Shrugging it off, she climbed into the driver's seat, started the car, and began her route back to the house.

Nearing the parking lot exit, she heard a loud whooshing sound above the car. Immediately, she hit the brakes and stopped the vehicle. Looking through the windshield to see what may have caused the sound, she asked Chase whether he had heard it too.

Chase, only five, asked, "What is a 'whooshing' sound?"

That question made Beth laugh a little. Grinning, she said, "It's the sound of a strong wind."

"No, I didn't hear anything, sissy. Is something wrong?"

"No. Everything is OK, little brother. I think the wind is just blowing hard. It's OK."

"OK, sissy."

"Ready to head home?" she asked Chase.

"Ready," he said, his face now covered with chocolate.

"All righty, let's go."

Feeling better, she turned on the radio and headed home. *First day here, and I'm ready to leave this place already*, she thought. *How am I going to last the whole weekend? Geez!* She sighed deeply.

"Why did they move so far out of town?" Beth asked herself. "I was hoping to get home before dark." She glanced in the rearview mirror at her little brother, who was fast asleep. "Awe, he's so precious; I just love him!"

Beth turned on the radio softly to occupy her time. *Well, imagine that! They have a decent radio* station here! she thought with a tone of sarcasm. She began singing along by turning up the music but not loud enough to wake Chase.

"Wow, where did this fog come from? It's getting hard to see where I'm going!" Beth said.

BAM!

Something big hit the car, causing her to lose control and crash into the ditch. "What the—?" she shouted. Not concerned about herself, she unbuckled and climbed over the front seat to get to her little brother. "Chase, are you OK?"

He looked up at her with widened eyes and asked, "Beth, what happened?"

"I'm not sure, but are you OK?"

He nodded and said, "Yes, sissy, I'm OK." She climbed back over the front seat, opened the door, and exited the car. "Stay in there, OK, little brother?"

"OK, Beth, I will."

Wanting to ensure the scene was safe, she scanned the area before walking too far from the car. "I guess it's OK; this fog makes it so hard to see!" she said. "OK, I don't see any danger. Is anyone out there?"

No one answered.

Beth slowly made her way to the front of the car to check the damage. The entire front of the vehicle was smashed like they had hit something significant. She looked at the car, then at the road. "What did I hit? There's nothing here!"

There was no sign of an animal, and they hadn't hit another car. Confused and extremely uneasy, she pulled out her phone to call for help, but there was no signal.

"Oh no! What do I do now? Why doesn't this stupid town have any cell towers?" she yelled. Feeling completely distraught, she remembered that her brother was still strapped into the car seat in the back. She returned to the car to check on him. "Chase, the car is damaged. We will wait inside for a little bit to see if a police officer comes by to help, OK?"

"OK."

Beth turned on the hazard lights, so if another vehicle passed by, the driver would know they were there on the road and not crash into them.

"How did the car get damaged, sissy?"

"I'm not sure, little brother, but everything will be OK." She looked at her phone. "It's eight o'clock already? It's going to be dark in a little bit. Well, I'm sure someone will drive by soon," she assured herself.

An hour passed, then two hours, and then …

"OK, we have to leave." Scared, tired, and concerned about her little brother, she opened the trunk to get his old stroller out. *He's a little big for it, but I can't carry him the rest of the way, so it'll have to do,* she thought.

"OK, buddy, looks like we're going to go on an adventure." She got him out of the car, placed him in the stroller, then made their way toward home on the dark, foggy road. "Hey, little dude," she said, "let's practice counting to one hundred."

"OK, sissy." This was her way of keeping him occupied and distracting her from the situation.

While walking toward the house with Melinie, Caleb suddenly became aware that something didn't feel right. It felt like something was watching them. "Move faster, Rachelle!"

They picked up their pace. "What the—?" Rachelle saw something large fly over them. "Oh, crap, it's here! Mel, wake up!" she shouted.

No response.

"Mel, please wake up!" she called again.

Melinie woke abruptly and said, "Where are we?"

"We're almost home, sis, but whatever took you is here!"

"OK, put me down; I think I can walk," Melinie responded.

Caleb lowered her from his shoulders to her feet. As she struggled to stand on her own, Rachelle noticed Mel's eyes widened with fear. She suddenly screamed, "Oh my God, no! It's above us!"

They all dropped low to the ground, hoping to avoid being taken by it. The creature stretched out its long arms to grab them; it missed.

"Look, it's coming back around!" Caleb screamed. "We've got to go now!"

Caleb and Rachelle jumped up quickly, sprinting toward the house. "Help!"

They spun around to find Melinie still on the ground, struggling to get up. Looking back at the sky, Caleb saw the creature heading straight for her. He ran toward her as fast as he could. Just as the beast was about to take her, he jumped toward Melinie, knocking her to the ground away from the creature. Knowing she was too weak to run alone, he threw her back over his shoulders, then ran toward the house.

Rachelle beat them there. She had the door open, waiting for them. With Melinie over his shoulders, he reached the front door, making it inside. As soon as they made it through, Rachelle closed the door. As Rachelle locked the door, the creature slammed into it, cracking it down the middle.

"Run to the basement!" Caleb yelled. They dashed there, deadbolted the door behind them, and cowered under the stairs.

"Where are Beth and Chase?" Melinie whimpered.

"They went to town to buy groceries a few hours ago, remember, and haven't made it home yet," said Rachelle.

"Something must have happened to them; we must find them!" cried Melinie.

"I know, but it's still out there, and you are in no condition to walk," said Caleb.

"I can make it; we have to go now!" yelled Melinie.

"We can't; we will have to wait!" said Caleb.

"We have to leave …" Mel passed out again. Wanting to find their siblings but paralyzed with fear, they stayed hidden.

This was Beth's first time in this little town. She had no idea how far it was back home. "Was it twenty miles or ten or more?" She had no clue. She looked at her phone to check the time. "11:05? So, we've been walking for about an hour without seeing a single car on the road; what the heck?" she said.

Noticing that Chase hadn't made a sound for a while, she looked in the stroller to find him fast asleep. This fact made her happy. Knowing he was comfortable enough to fall asleep must be a good sign, though she wished he was awake so she could have someone to talk to. Yeah, he was only five, but it would be a little less nerve wracking to have someone to talk to. *Well, at least the fog has lightened up some!* she thought. *I can see where I'm going.*

Needing a distraction, she thought, *Maybe I'll hum some songs; that'll help.* She began humming nursery rhymes. "Why am I humming nursery rhymes?" she asked herself. "Of all the songs I have listened to and love, why nursery rhymes? I must be losing it!" She rolled her eyes and laughed.

As she continued walking on the dark, lonely road while pushing Chase in his stroller, something caught her attention. On the opposite side of the highway, she saw what appeared to be a glowing circle on a tree. Stopping for a minute to get a better look, she said, "That looks like a big, red eye! How weird is that? It must be a marker of some sort that the farmers put on the trees, and the moon must shine on it to make it glow. Wait, where is the moon?" She picked up the pace.

Nearly at a jogger's pace now, she decided to take another look. Glancing back, she saw that what she had figured was a marker earlier was now gone. *That's strange!* she thought. Turning around, she saw the same feature glowing on another tree farther down the road in the direction she was heading. Her heart began to beat faster.

Should I wake Chase up? she wondered. *No, I must get him home as fast as possible.*

She looked at her phone again. *Nearly midnight. The sun won't be up for another few hours*, she thought. *We need to find a ride home!*

The fog quickly rolled back in, and she could no longer see down the road. "What is up with this fog? I've never seen fog like this! Must be a country thing!" Beth whispered. Scared and frustrated, she looked at the sky and quietly said, "Please send someone to help us!"

Suddenly she was lifted into the air, then dropped hard onto the pavement. Her body writhed in pain. It hurt to move. "Chase!" she screamed. "Where are you?"

"Beth!" he yelled.

Beth heard her little brother crying, but she didn't see him.

"Sissy!" he screamed.

When she looked around to find him, something grabbed her feet and tossed her back into the air. She landed face-first in the ditch. She screamed in agony from the painful landing. Barely able to move, she managed to turn over with her body facing the night sky.

Struggling to open her eyes, she became blinded by a powerful red light. It was so bright that her eyes felt like they were on fire. Screaming in pain, she covered her eyes to avoid the painful light.

Keeping her eyes covered, she screamed for Chase again. "Sissy, help!" she heard him scream. While shielding her eyes, Beth painfully managed to get to her feet. Desperate to find her brother despite the pain, she removed her hands from her eyes to look for him.

Everything was blurry from the blinding light. Continuing to look, her eyes slowly focused but not good enough to see clearly. Hearing something close to her, she strained her eyes to make it out. She could distinguish what appeared to be a face. Wrongfully assuming it was her brother, she reached out to him.

There was a deep growl. It wasn't her brother. She immediately withdrew her hands, quickly scrambling away.

As she moved farther back, her eyes came into focus. She was face-to-face with something awful that looked right at her. Its face resembled that of a disfigured man. It had one large eye in the center of its body that glowed red, and it had giant wings. She realized instantly that it was this creature's eye she had seen on the trees.

The unknown beast stared at her and unfurled one of its wings to show her it had her brother wrapped inside it. It smirked at her, then lifted in the air to fly away with her brother.

Forgetting the pain, Beth grabbed a large piece of asphalt that had broken away from the road and tried throwing it at the winged creature. As she lifted her arm to throw it, the creature flew at her quickly, knocking her backward onto the road and causing her to hit her head. The impact of the road knocked her unconscious.

Chase called to his sister for help as he was taken away, but his screams didn't wake her up.

Wincing from the bright light, Rachelle slowly opened her eyes to find the sun peeking through the basement window. "Hey guys, wake up!" she said. "We fell asleep, and the sun is up. Do you think it's gone?"

Melinie and Caleb rubbed their eyes. "It's morning?" asked Melinie.

"Yes!" said Rachelle. "We made it through."

"Do you think it's still out there?" asked Caleb.

"I'm too afraid to look!" said Rachelle.

"Well, we must check because we still need to find out what happened to Beth and Chase," said Melinie. Caleb and Rachelle nodded in agreement. They all climbed out from under the staircase, then slowly and cautiously began walking up the stairs; their eyes darting back and forth for any signs of whatever was after them.

Arriving at the top of the stairs, they looked at one another, mentally asking, *Who will be the first to open the door?* Finally, when her siblings didn't offer to be first in line, Rachelle turned the doorknob, then slowly opened the door ever so slightly.

Feeling like her heart would explode from beating so fast, she pushed against the door, waiting for it to open before peeking her head out to look around. With no immediate signs of danger, she paused a minute longer to listen for anything in the house. "I think it's OK to come up," she said. Waiting a few seconds more to build up enough bravery to enter the hallway, she finally did so.

Still apprehensive, she looked both ways, doing her best to see as far down each direction as she could before taking another step. Caleb quietly said, "Do you see anything, Rachelle?"

"No," she said. "I think we're good." Hoping she was right, Melinie and Caleb stepped through the doorway, joining Rachelle in the hallway.

Trembling with fear, they slowly searched the entire house to ensure they were alone; the place was empty, excluding something that scurried over Melinie's foot, causing her to scream. "What is it?" Caleb asked, fearing the worst.

"Uh-uh, nothing. It was just a mouse," she said as she shrugged, then smiled in embarrassment. Caleb looked at her awkwardly; then, they both broke into laughter.

"Geez, Melinie, I'm not sure what scared you more, the creature or the mouse?" he said.

"Well, mice are pretty scary too." Melinie laughed.

Rachelle had been on the other side of the house when she heard Melanie scream, which caused her to run into the kitchen. Out of breath, she asked what had happened. Laughing, they told Rachelle. Rachelle was in no mood to play around; she wasn't amused.

"OK, I'm glad you got a second to laugh about our situation, but it's time we make a game plan. Do you think it's possible that it only comes out at night?" Rachelle asked.

"Well, only one way to find out," Caleb added. "Someone needs to open the front door. Rachelle, are you feeling brave enough?"

"What? Why me?" she asked.

"Figured since you opened the basement door, you may want to be the one to open the front door, too," Caleb said with a whimsical smile.

"Are you for real?" she asked.

"Of course not! Just trying to lighten the mood a little."

"It's not helping," she said.

"Sorry! OK, you guys, get ready; I'm going to open the door," Caleb said. "Please only come out at night! Please only come out at night!" he repeated as he headed for the front door. "Well, here we go!"

Figuring it would be best to get it done quickly, Caleb unlocked the door and kicked it open. Because of the damage the door had incurred from the creature slamming into it the night before, it nearly fell off its hinges.

Experiencing an odd feeling of confidence, he leaped onto the porch, landing in a fighting position and letting out his most ferocious growl. To his pleasant surprise, there was no monster to fight.

"Come out! It's all clear!" he shouted to his sisters.

They walked out of the house and onto the porch. "Nice job, Caleb! I think your mighty growl might have scared it away," Melinie said, patting his back and laughing. He shrugged and let out a confident smile.

The sun felt so good on their faces. For a moment, they forgot about the horrific night they had just experienced and bathed in the sun's warmth. "What now?" asked Rachelle.

In unison, both Caleb and Melinie let out a deep sigh. The unfortunate reality of their situation crept back in; they knew time wasn't on their side. They had to focus on finding Beth and Chase.

"First, we get a few supplies. Then get off this property and find Beth and Chase," Rachelle said. "We know they were in town buying groceries, so we head that way."

Melinie and Caleb nodded in agreement. They packed a few supplies in their backpacks and walked toward the road.

Still lying on the road, Beth heard, "Are you OK?" An unfamiliar voice asked, "Ma'am, are you OK? Do you need help?"

Beth opened her eyes, feeling so disoriented. She tried to stand up, but the pain from her fall caused her to collapse onto the pavement. Suddenly, she remembered what had happened last night and screamed, "Chase!"

"Ma'am? Are you hurt?" the voice asked again.

Managing to get to a sitting position, she saw a young man standing next to her with concern in his eyes. She looked at him and asked, "Have you seen my little brother?"

The young man replied, "Sorry, I haven't seen anybody except you. What happened? Is that your wrecked car down the road?"

She nodded. "My brother and I were driving home last night when something hit the car. We were trying to walk home when something attacked me and took him. He's only five; we must find him!" she cried with tears.

"I'm so sorry, ma'am!" he said. "There isn't any cell service out here, but I live only about a mile down the road. I have a landline. We can drive to my house and call the sheriff if you can move."

"Yes, thank you!" They got into his car, then headed to the young man's house.

Caleb, Melinie, and Rachelle reached the road, intending to walk to town. Stopping at the edge of their driveway, they looked at each other. "Do either of you know which way to go?" Caleb asked, realizing that they had no idea whether the town was to the right or the left. There weren't any road signs at the junction by their house, and none had noticed how they had gotten there when their parents drove there from town.

"Which way do we go?" asked Melinie.

Caleb and Rachelle shrugged, having no idea. "Let's stand by the road for a few minutes to see if anyone drives by," said Rachelle. Agreeing to wait, they stood at the edge of the driveway, expecting a car to pass by at any moment so they could get to town.

Nearing the young man's house, Beth realized she hadn't asked his name. "So, I'm Beth, by the way."

"Oh, I'm Zack."

"Nice to meet you, Zack. Thank you for helping me."

"You're welcome, Beth; I'm just glad I was driving your way so I could help."

"Me too, Zack!"

"Well, here we are, Beth."

Beth looked at the house; it was an old farmhouse. It was a bit run down, but anywhere felt safer than being stuck on the road alone.

"Are your parents' home, Zack?"

"This is my place, and I live alone. Probably going to get a dog someday so I can have some company and not be stuck talking to myself," he said, chuckling a little.

"Yeah, I get that," said Beth.

"I bought it from my uncle, who was getting too old to care for it. I know it's a little worn down, but it's my first home. I plan to fix it up and get the farm operating again."

"That's pretty awesome," said Beth.

"Thank you!" Zack responded. "All right, let's go inside and call the sheriff."

As they walked from the car to Zack's house, a strange thick fog started rolling in rapidly. "Whoa!" Zack said. "Where did that come from? It's been clear all day."

Feeling a little unnerved, Beth said, "I'm not sure, but maybe we should hurry before it gets to us." Zack agreed as they picked up their pace.

Caleb, Melinie, and Rachelle continued waiting on the roadside, hoping someone would come by. "Hey, look!" Rachelle yelled. "There's a car coming."

"Finally!" Caleb said. Each of them began waving his or her hands in the air, trying to get the driver's attention. As the car drew closer, a deep fog rolled in from nowhere. It was so thick they were no longer able to see the vehicle approaching them.

"Do you see the car?" asked Melinie.

"No!" said Caleb.

"The fog is too thick," Rachelle responded.

Hoping the vehicle was still headed their way, they turned on their flashlights and began waving them, hoping the driver would see them. The car never came into sight.

Whoosh!

"The creature's in the fog!" screamed Melinie.

"Get off the road and turn off your flashlights!" Rachelle said softly. Quickly, the flashlights went off, and they jumped into the ditch, hiding inside the tall grass. Moments later, they heard a muffled scream somewhere inside the fog.

"Do you think it got them?" Rachelle whispered. Neither Melinie nor Caleb responded, but they already knew that was likely the case. They could only wait and hope they wouldn't be seen.

"Should we run, Caleb?" Melinie asked.

"I don't think we have a choice. I'm sure it knows we're here, and we are just sitting ducks if we stay. On three, let's run to the house, OK?" said Caleb.

"OK," Rachelle said.

"Sounds good," Melinie responded. "OK, one … two …"

Before Caleb could say three, they heard a blood-curdling scream from within the fog again. Paralyzed with fear, none of them got up to run. Instead, they just lay there, wondering if they would be next.

As quickly as it came, the scream ended. Moments later, the fog completely dissipated. With the fog gone, they could see down the road but couldn't tell if the car was still there.

"We have to see if they're OK," Caleb said.

"Are you flipping crazy?" asked Melinie. "What if this is a trap?"

Knowing she was probably right; Caleb still couldn't fight his inner instincts to check anyways. "It might be, but what if they're hurt? No one else is here to help."

"The car isn't even there!" said Melinie.

"It might be in the ditch, and we can't see it. I've got to go."

"OK, but we're going with you," said Rachelle.

"You're both insane!" Melinie told them.

"Fine! We'll go, but if no one is there, please promise we'll return to the house."

"I promise," Caleb responded. They hurried down the road, looking around constantly for any signs of the creature.

There were no signs of the car or its passengers when they arrived. "Look at this!" said Rachelle. There were long skid marks on the road, not the usual kind from a car hitting its brakes, but it looked like it had been dragged sideways off the road.

"Where's the car?" asked Caleb.

"I don't know, but it's not here, and neither are any people, so let's go!" Melinie said in a very commanding tone.

"Look at this!" Rachelle said. There were shards of glass and metal pieces strewn all over the road. "I think it took them and the car, too."

"I think you're right!" Caleb said.

"OK, so we know that it took them. We also know there's nothing we can do. So, can we go now, Caleb?" Melinie said in a pleading tone.

"Yeah, let's get out of here before it returns." They left the scene and headed straight to the house.

"I can't take this!" screamed Melinie once they were inside.

"Why is this happening?" asked Rachelle.

"I don't know," said Caleb, "But we can't stay here."

"It's not going to let us leave," said Rachelle. "I don't know why, but the only safe place seems to be the basement."

"Well then, let's go back downstairs and wait it out," said Melinie.

Based on their experience, this was the only idea that made sense. "Rachelle, grab some drinks," Melinie said. "Caleb, grab some food, and I'll grab some kitchen knives and whatever else I can find to take down there. If you're right, Rachelle, we might be down there for a while and need to eat and drink. If you're wrong, hopefully, the knives will be useful if we need to defend ourselves; Lord, I hope you're right!"

After gathering the supplies, they headed back downstairs and gathered under the basement staircase.

Fog overtook the home when Beth and Zack reached the front door. Reaching into his pants pocket, Zack pulled out his keys. The fog was so thick that he couldn't find the front door key. "Hurry!" yelled Beth.

"I'm trying!" yelled Zack. Deciding to try every key, he finally found the right one; they opened the door, stepped inside, and slammed the door. For good measure, Zack locked the door behind him.

Zack sighed in relief as he leaned against the door. "Geez, that fog came out of nowhere!" he told Beth. "Beth, are you OK?"

Beth didn't say a word. All the blood had drained from her face. White as a ghost, she appeared to be in a trance as she stared wide eyed at the front door. "What's wrong, Beth?" he asked nervously.

"Something is outside; I can feel it," she whispered.

"How do you know?" he asked, his voice cracking.

"I feel it," she whispered again. Zack walked toward her and put his hand on her shoulder to turn her away from the door. Suddenly, there was a knock at the door.

Startled, they both looked at the door. *Knock, knock, knock.* There it was again. Zack asked, mustering as much courage as he could, "Who is it?"

There was no response.

Zack walked straight to the kitchen, opened the drawer, and pulled out a pistol. "Beth, stay behind me," he said as he made his way to the front door. Beth grabbed his shoulder and walked with him, scared beyond anything she had ever felt.

Zack lifted the gun, aiming it at the center of the door, then shouted, "Who's there?"

Nothing but silence.

"Beth, I'm going to open the door. Be prepared to run and hide if something goes wrong."

"Are you kidding me?" Beth said, her voice trembling.

"Don't be afraid, Beth; I won't let anything hurt you."

"Listen to me, Zack! Something is out there; I've seen it. It's huge, it has wings, and it took my brother. I don't think a gun is going to kill it!"

"Well, we can't just wait for whatever it is to attack us or play on our fear," Zach responded.

Beth continued to press the issue, pleading with him not to open the door, but he was determined to get the first shot before it could strike. Finally, realizing Zack wouldn't listen to reason, Beth said, "OK, but do it slowly, and please be careful!" Zack nodded in agreement.

Keeping the pistol pointed toward the door's centerline, he unlocked it, turned the knob, then slowly opened the door. Zack had seen enough movies to know he needed to keep his body inside to prevent an intruder or whatever else from gaining the upper hand. Keeping his finger on the trigger, Zack kicked the door open. Standing ready to take on the intruder, he stood there momentarily, waiting for something or someone to enter the doorway, but there was no sign of an intruder, or the terrifying monster Beth had described.

Cautiously, with the pistol still in position, he looked around in each direction; no sign of what had made the knocking sound. *Maybe it was some kids playing a prank or possibly a woodpecker*, Zack thought. *Either way, there's nothing or no one outside.* Feeling somewhat at ease but choosing to stay on guard, Zack walked backward from off the front porch and headed through the front door, staying in a ready position, just in case.

After stepping back through the doorway, he turned toward Beth to share the good news. "You can relax now, Beth; we are safe from the flying creature."

Beth didn't like his sarcastic tone. "You don't have to believe me, Zack, but what I told you was true. Just get back in here so we can call the sheriff!"

Zack hung his head, knowing he had offended her. "Beth, I'm sorry. I shouldn't have …" He felt the hairs on his neck stand up. He looked at Beth, then turned around quickly, lifting his pistol to defend himself. Immediately, his eyes were blinded by a red light. Dropping his gun to shield his eyes with his hands, he stumbled forward and out onto the porch.

Still covering his eyes, he was made deaf with an intense and excruciating scream, which burst his eardrums and caused blood to run down his jawline. His knees buckled from the pain, causing him to fall onto the porch floor. Crying out in pain, Zack was entirely overcome by the creature's scream.

Beth stood there, frozen, watching it all unfold. Unable to scream or move, she was paralyzed and helpless. As she watched, the creature lowered itself from the porch roof. First appeared its head, which was turned toward her, keeping its eyes fixed on her. Using its claws, it slowly climbed down the walls until its entire body was on the porch, standing over Zack.

The creature wrapped Zack up in its wings, looked at Beth with an insidious stare, then ascended into the sky. Like her little brother, Chase, Zack was taken away from her.

Beth dropped to the floor, put her head between her knees, and cried uncontrollably. "Why is this happening? Where is my brother? What have I done to deserve this?" she sobbed. "Someone, please help me! *Help me!*"

CHAPTER 2

MARK AND AMBER

"Hon, don't you think we should forget about this weekend trip and stay with the kids?" Amber asked Mark.

"Nah, they'll be fine! Besides, I asked my friend Jay to stop by and check on them."

"I know, but I feel uncomfortable leaving them with no way to contact us; I wish we had the Wi-Fi set up, you know?"

"I get it," said Mark. "They don't work on the weekends. I'll call to set it up first thing in the morning. I think they'll survive one weekend without it."

"OK, but if I feel something is wrong, we're heading back," Amber said sternly.

"Well. Of course!" said Mark. "Look, we haven't had a chance in a long time to get away; we deserve some time to relax. Everything will be fine."

"OK, but remember, one weird feeling, and—"

Mark cut her off. "Yeah, and relax time is out the window. I know," he said with a frustrated tone.

It was about midday the following day when Jay remembered that he needed to check on Mark and Amber's kids. Jay grabbed his keys and headed to their small home about twenty miles from town. Mark had been Jay's best friend for nearly forty years.

As he drove, he began reminiscing about all the good times they'd had together as kids. Mid-memory of their eighth-grade basketball tournament, he came upon a wrecked car in the opposite lane. He didn't recognize the vehicle, but for some strange reason, it made him think about Mark's kids; seeing that it had been involved in an accident caused him great concern.

Deciding it was best to check it out, he pulled over to examine the scene to see whether anyone was inside. When he arrived, he saw that the car had been hit hard in the front; maybe there had been a head-on collision with another car or a deer, but there was no sign of another vehicle or an injured animal that had caused the damage.

Stepping out of his car, he hurried to the driver's side of the wrecked vehicle. When he arrived, the driver's side door and rear passenger door, along with the trunk, were all open, but no one was inside.

He checked the roadside and ditch; no one was in either place. *I guess whoever it was must be gone or received help from someone*, he figured.

Before leaving, he took one more peek inside the car in case he had missed something about the occupants. *Nothing up front*, he thought. Glancing in the back, he found an empty car seat. *Mark's youngest is around five and would probably be in a car seat. This is serious*, he thought. *Should I drive home and call the sheriff or continue to his house to check on the kids?* he wondered. Thinking it was more important to check on the kids, he ran back to the car, then sped off to their house.

Jay had given up his cell phone for a satellite phone some time ago. He had concluded that a cell phone was just an expensive waste of money without cell towers. Reaching into his front pocket, he pulled out his satellite phone to dial Mark's number. Looking at the phone's screen, he noticed it was trying to locate a satellite to connect with.

"What the—?" Jay was annoyed. "It never takes this long to find a satellite. Come on, stupid phone!" he yelled. "This is not a good time to be glitchy!" He felt very anxious and needed to get ahold of Mark.

Jay pulled off to the side of the road, got out, and lifted the phone in every direction, trying to get a signal. He kept this up for several minutes but failed. *Well, I can't wait out here forever,* he thought. He returned to the car, driving as fast as he could to the house.

"Why is this taking so long?" he asked loudly. Jay pushed harder on the gas pedal to gain more speed; instead, the car slowed down. He smashed the pedal to the floor; the car slowed down even more. Jay looked down at the gauges to see why he was slowing down; nothing appeared wrong.

There are no warning lights on. Everything is good, he thought. "Plenty of gas. The battery and temp are fine. What is going on?" he yelled in frustration. "Is my motor shot? Guess I'll drop it off at the mechanics on Monday!"

Looking up from the gauges, he saw their driveway coming into view. "I made it. Geez that took forever!" he exclaimed. Jay turned on his left blinker to turn into the driveway. Then: "Wait, what's happening?" he shouted.

The driveway began to move farther away like he is driving backward. "Whoa, what the …?" Jay slammed on the brakes to stop the car from rolling back away from the house, and the vehicle stopped.

Jay put the car in park. *What is going on? Something isn't right,* he thought. Goose bumps covered his arms; the hair on his neck stood up. Feeling that he wasn't alone and sensing a strange evil presence that he couldn't explain, Jay sat very still in his car, his eyes darting back and forth, looking, and hoping that it was just a feeling and that there was nothing there to be concerned about.

"I don't see anything outside," Jay said to himself. Concluding that he was probably scared for nothing, he stepped out of the car. *I guess I'm walking from here,* he thought.

A thick fog began covering the road after he had closed the car door. "Where did that come from?" Jay reached back for the car handle to get inside, but he couldn't find the car; it wasn't there. Blinded by the fog, he kept looking for the vehicle without success. He also looked for the driveway to Mark's house, but the fog hid it. Surrounded by fog and not understanding what was happening, Jay felt helpless.

What is going on? he wondered, fearing what might be in the fog with him. His heart began to race. Fear was taking him over.

"Get it together, Jay," he whispered, scolding himself for freaking out. "It's just fog!" Jay touched the ground to ensure he was on the asphalt. "Yep, that's pavement. As long as I don't get off the road, I can navigate to their driveway."

Jay continued walking down the road, taking a few steps at a time, then checking to ensure it was pavement. "Once I get close, I should be able to see through the fog enough to find his driveway," he assured himself.

After just a few steps, Jay heard a strange scratching sound. It brought back memories of someone scratching his or her fingernails on the chalkboard in the classroom at school. He had always hated that sound, but he wasn't at school, and there wasn't a chalkboard to scratch; he was all alone in the fog.

What could it be? Jay wondered as the goose bumps on his arms came back. "Dude, you're in the country! That could be a bird, a squirrel, or another little animal. Stop tripping out!" he told himself.

The scratching sound stopped.

"See, you're worried about nothing," Jay said to comfort himself. "And why am I talking to myself?" He laughed a little. "Good thing Mark's not here; he'd be razzing me like crazy!"

After he took a few more steps, the sound came back. Then there was the sound of glass shattering. No longer convinced that he was scared for no reason, he began running as fast as he could in the direction he hoped was toward Mark's house.

With each stride, he stumbled over something in the road, causing him to fall. Each time he fell, he'd get back up and continue to run with all he had. Falling one more time, he noticed he was on gravel. He also saw a mailbox.

"Please be Mark's!" he pleaded. It was. "I made it!" he yelled. Taking a deep breath, he jumped up quickly to sprint the rest of the way.

Bam!

He slammed face-first into something hard.

Jay cried out in pain and immediately grabbed his nose. "I think it's broken!" he exclaimed. *What did I run into? Did Mark put up a wall?* he wondered. With one hand still on his nose, he extended the other to feel for the object he had run into. "What is this? It doesn't feel like a fence!"

Trying his best to wipe the blood away, which was now draining down his face from his broken nose, he kept touching the invisible object to figure out what it was.

"Where's the opening?" he shouted. Frantically, he kept feeling the area for an opening. He bent down to touch the ground beneath his feet. "It's gravel. I'm still in their driveway!" While he kept looking, the fog lifted enough for him to see their house. "There it is! I'm in their driveway for sure! Why can't I get through?"

Keeping his hand on the invisible barrier, he tried walking around it to find a way through. "Come on, why can't I find a way through?" Jay shouted.

Feeling hopeless, he called, "Help! Someone, help me!"

"Say my name!" an unfamiliar voice said in a deep, gravelly voice.

"Who's there?" Jay asked.

"Say my name!" the voice said again but louder.

"Who are you?" Jay said, fear gripping him.

"I am he who is unseen, he whose name is unwritten."

Jay cried, "Please, don't hurt—"

He was immediately silenced. The creature wrapped its wings around his body, driving the air from his lungs. Even though he was in the driveway and only a stone's throw away from the house, Mark's children didn't hear his cries for help.

Before snatching Jay away, the creature sank its elongated teeth into his neck, draining enough blood to feed but not enough to take his life. Moments later, the creature took him away and flew into the sky.

Sitting on the bed in the hotel room, Mark looked down at his watch. *I haven't heard from Jay regarding the kids. I'll give him a call, just to make sure everything is OK.* He thought.

Mark dialed Jay's number. "That's weird; it's not ringing," he said quietly. He tried his number again.

A recorded voice said, "The party you are trying to reach is unavailable at this time; please try your call again later." Mark tried Jay's number several more times; the same recorded message came on the line each time.

"Mark!" Amber said.

"Yes?" Mark responded.

"Have you heard anything from Jay yet regarding the kids?"

"No, not yet," replied Mark. "I'll check in about an hour, OK?" He started to worry a little but didn't want to scare Amber, so he didn't tell her about being unable to reach Jay. *No reason to concern her. I'm sure everything is fine; maybe his satellite phone isn't getting a signal*, he thought. *I'll give it another hour, then try again.*

An hour came and went. Mark redialed his number. "Hey, it's ringing!" Mark said quietly with a sigh of relief. After three or four rings, the call was connected, but there was silence on the other end. "Jay?" asked Mark.

There was no reply.

"Jay, can you hear me?"

Again, there was only silence.

"Jay!" shouted Mark. "Are you there?"

Amber was in the hotel bathroom and heard Mark shouting on the phone. She rushed out of the bathroom and into the main room to see why he was shouting. "Mark, what's going on?"

"I'm on the phone with Jay, but he's not answering. The call is connected, but I guess something is wrong with the signal."

"Put it on speaker so I can see if I can hear him," Amber told Mark. He put the phone on speaker, trying again to communicate with Jay.

"Jay, can you hear—"

Before he could finish his sentence, a loud, bone-chilling voice said, "Yes, I hear you."

Mark looked at Amber; she looked back, and both felt the cold chills of absolute horror. With her voice shaking with fear, Amber asked, "Who is this?"

"I am he who is unseen, he whose name is unwritten," the voice responded.

Amber looked at Mark with tears running down her cheeks. "Jay, this isn't funny!"

"Are the kids with you?" Mark shouted.

The voice didn't respond.

"Jay, are you there?"

"He is with me! I see your children!" the voice said.

"Please, don't hurt our children!" Amber cried.

"What do you want?" asked Mark.

"Say my name," the voice demanded.

"OK, tell me your name, and I'll say it. Just don't hurt our children!" Mark replied.

"*Say my name!*" the voice shouted with a God-awful scream.

Amber grabbed the phone from Mark's hands. "What is your name?"

Silence. She looked at the phone; the screen was black. "Mark, the phone is dead or something."

"Hand it to me," Mark responded. She complied. He tried to turn the phone back on, but it wouldn't power up. Immediately, he grabbed the charger and plugged it into the wall outlet. It came on for a second, then powered off. He pressed the power button again.

This time it powered on but became extremely hot. Mark tried to let go of the phone, and immediately it melted onto his skin. Mark screamed in agony, pulling at it to get it off his hand. "Amber, help me!" he cried.

Amber tried to grab the phone, but it burned her, too. "Ouch! I can't touch it, Mark!"

"Get some water!" he said.

Amber retrieved a cup of water from the bathroom sink. Running back to Mark as fast as possible, she poured it over the phone.

A loud evil scream blasted through the phone's speaker. The sound from the phone caused the room to shake as if they were in an earthquake. Mark and Amber were violently thrown to the ground. Unable to stand, with the phone still burning Mark's flesh, the phone screeched, then fell to the floor. The shaking and screaming stopped, but Mark cried in pain.

Still dizzy from the turbulent shaking, Amber made her way to Mark. "Let me see your hand, Mark! Oh, Lord, that is bad! We need to get you to the hospital."

"No! Just grab the first aid kit. I have some burn cream and gauze inside the kit. Just treat the burn and wrap it up. We must get to the kids!"

"Mark! That's a severe burn. We need to get you to the ER immediately!"

"And how do we explain my hand getting burned so bad? We can't, and they would think we're crazy. No, I'll be fine. Besides, our kids cannot wait. I'll see a doctor afterward; we must get to the kids."

"Mark!" Amber said with deep concern.

"Come on, get the kit, Amber!"

She knew that once Mark had made up his mind, she would have no chance of changing it. Plus, she realized he was right in what he had said; there was no logical way to explain what had just happened. She ran to the car and returned with the first aid kit to treat his wounds.

"Good enough! Let's go!" Mark said. Leaving their suitcases and belongings in the hotel room, they sped off toward home. "Amber, call the sheriff."

Amber reached into her pocket for her phone; it wasn't there. "I think it's still in the hotel room," she said.

"Well, we can't go back now; We're an hour away from the hotel," Mark said.

"Mark, we're eight hours from home; what will we do? What if that person has our children?" she asked, sobbing.

"We just keep driving until we see a police station, a police car, or a pay phone," said Mark. Extremely upset, he tried his best to devise any words that might comfort her. He wanted to assure her that the kids would be OK, but he couldn't find any reassurance, so he kept silent. Unable to do anything but wipe the tears from his eyes so he could see the road, he remained silent as he raced down the highway.

Amber broke the silence after they didn't say a word to each other for several miles. "Mark, what just happened? How did the phone get hot enough to burn you? Who was that on the other end of the line? How is any of this possible?"

"It's not! I can't explain what just happened. It's not possible!"

"But it happened, Mark? Look at your hand! Those are serious burns. How can a person do that?"

Mark didn't respond. He had no explanation to give Amber, and she didn't push further to get one from him either. They both knew no person could make things like that happen. And what about the room shaking? He had no answers, only questions. Getting to the kids was the only thing on his mind.

Mark and Amber were different from what you would call the religious type. If they were anything, they considered themselves to lean more toward agnostic. However, out of hopeless desperation, Mark mouthed a silent petition. "God, if you're there, please protect my children!" This was his first time sending out such a plea. He hoped that if there were a God or some higher power, perhaps it would hear his inadequate prayers and see fit to protect his children long enough for him to get to them.

CHAPTER 3

SEE ME

After hours of crying on Zach's living room floor, Beth realized no one was coming to help her. She was on her own and all alone. Nothing she'd ever experienced could have prepared her for what she had gone through.

No person should ever suffer this way, she thought. She pulled her knees to her chest, and with her head down, she started crying again. Lost in the tragedy of what had happened to Zack, she didn't realize the door was still open. Slowly gaining her composure, she suddenly felt like something was there with her. Her instincts told her to open her eyes and look up, but she was terrified.

"This isn't real! I've lost my mind. This is a delusion of some kind!" she whispered, rocking back and forth as she kept her eyes shut. Just then, she heard sounds of heavy breathing; she still didn't look up or open her eyes. The breathing continued, and now she could feel the breath moving the hair on her head from the exhalation. Shaking her head, she continued her mantra that this wasn't real.

Hoping she would wake up from this nightmare, she heard a deep growl and a voice say, "Look at me, Beth!" This forced her to lift her head just a little. She was still too afraid to open her eyes. "See me!" the voice shouted.

Shaking severely, she managed to open her eyes and see the feet of the creature speaking to her. They were like a person's feet but also appeared like goat hooves with long, talon-like claws. Refusing to look at what was attached to its feet, Beth crawled backward as fast as she could, screaming until she could finally stand up and run to the kitchen, slipping behind the counter to hide.

After a few minutes of hiding, she peeked over the counter; nothing appeared to be chasing her. Not feeling safe enough to come out of hiding, Beth pulled a knife out of one of the kitchen drawers to defend herself.

Nothing was coming after her but was it safe to come out? she wondered. Inhaling deeply, she halfway stood up to peek over the counter. Nothing was in the house, but due to the house's design, she couldn't see around the kitchen corner and into the living room to see the front door. Holding her breath for a minute to listen for the creature to make noise, she could hear only the hard thump of her heart beating rapidly.

I have to get closer, Beth thought. Taking only baby steps, she passed through the kitchen until the living room came into view. Something was standing in the doorway to the outdoors. She could hear it breathing but could only make out its silhouette due to the surrounding fog. It had the shape of a large man, but it was no man.

Suddenly images of her little brother flooded her head. Her fear transitioned to anger. Her anger turned to rage. Suddenly empowered by her new emotions, she yelled, "Where is my brother?"

The creature just stood there.

Feeling braver, she walked closer and yelled again, "Where is my brother? Give him back to me!"

The creature didn't respond but began to growl. Feeling that somehow, she was protected inside the house, she walked toward the open door until she was an arm's length from it, then yelled even louder, "Where is my brother? Give him back!"

The creature responded with a scream, extended its enormous wings, then flew straight up.

Nearly falling back from fright, Beth ran back to the kitchen. Not hearing anything for a minute, she asked herself, "Is it gone?" Cautiously, she walked back to the front door, listening and waiting for any sign of the creature. She looked outside; the fog was still there.

Does that mean it's still here waiting for me? she wondered. *What do I do?*

Trying to be as calculated as possible, she stayed still until she came up with a safe answer to her question. *If I go outside, I have no chance. If I stay in here, will it wait me out?* she wondered. *There is no good option, and I'm probably dead either way.*

Beth scanned the room for an answer. *I can't believe it!* Zack's gun was on the floor next to where the creature had stood. *He must have dropped it when the creature grabbed him,* she figured. *I need to get it!*

Grabbing the nearest thing she could find; she found a large pot. She planned to throw it at the beast if it returned to the door to distract it so she could get to the gun.

As she approached the front door to grab the gun, the beast reappeared in the doorway. She immediately threw the pot at its head, hitting it. Getting hit by the pot stunned the creature long enough for her to grab the gun. Once she had it, she sprinted back into the kitchen, hearing the creature scream as she ran.

"Do I remember the training my dad gave me?" She checked the clip; it was fully loaded. Once she had snapped the clip back in place, her dad's training kicked in immediately. Armed with a fully loaded weapon, she was ready to unload it on the monster that had taken her brother and Zack. Beth headed back toward the door, feeling brave with the pistol securely positioned.

Coming within arm's length of the front door, Beth yelled to the creature, "Come get me." At that moment, the creature's whole form appeared before her. Beth unloaded on the beast without hesitating until "Click, click, click." The gun was empty.

Did I get it? she wondered. Scanning the whole area for any signs of blood, she saw and heard nothing. No sounds of whimpering or cries telling of an injury from the gunshots. Her plan to at least injure the creature seemed to have failed. She now stood there with an unloaded gun, her courage fading away. As she trembled, fear came in like a flood, terrorizing her thoughts.

"The knife!" Beth ran back to the kitchen and grabbed the knife she had pulled out of the drawer earlier.

Beth walked again to the front door, this time with the knife. *Where is it?* she wondered.

Then suddenly, the creature appeared. Its huge frame filled the entire doorway again. "Where is my brother?" she shouted. "Do you hear me? Where is my brother?"

Just as Beth thought about stabbing the creature, she noticed it was standing completely still but looking up at something. *What is it doing?* she wondered. "Hey, I'm right here!"

The creature continued looking at the top of the doorframe, ignoring her.

I've had enough of this! she thought. With a loud shout, she screamed at the beast, "What do you want!"

It lowered its gaze from the top of the door, stretching its neck forward through the fog, allowing her to see its face. Looking straight at her, it screamed, "Say my name!"

The creature's voice somehow projected images in her head. She saw a young man being tormented in a dark place. His tormentor was a shadowy image she couldn't describe. Over and over, she heard the young man scream, but no one came to help him. Before he collapsed to the floor, her final images were bite marks on the young man's torso and blood on his mouth.

The images were too intense to handle, causing her to pass out. However, as her body was losing consciousness, she was awake long enough to see the entity take another look at the top of the door. Then, with a deep-throated growl, it spread its wings upward and vanished from her sight.

CHAPTER 4

THE BASEMENT

Beth's siblings remained huddled together under the basement stairs. Even though the creature was still outside and hadn't entered any part of the house, they felt that staying in the basement was their best and safest option.

Too afraid to speak, they didn't utter a single word the entire time; they were worried the creature would hear them talking and find a way to get them. Finally, breaking the silence, Rachelle piped up and said, "Why do you think it hasn't come inside?"

Melinie and Caleb looked at her in a way she could tell meant, *Don't even go there!* So, she kept quiet. After a while, Rachelle grew tired of the silence; she whispered, "Mel, can I ask you a question?"

"Sure, Rachelle, but do it quietly."

"OK. What happened in your room, and how did you get under the ground?"

Melinie looked at her, then down momentarily as if trying to collect herself enough to respond. Looking back at her, she quietly began recounting what she could remember. "I was sitting on the bed, listening to music, when I saw what I thought was a bird flying and passing the window. I didn't think much of it until I heard pecking at the window. Curious, I walked over to the window to see what it was, but it stopped. Not thinking much of it, I was walking back to the bed when out of the corner of my eye, I saw a bright red light flashing in front of the window.

"It caught my attention, and I walked back to the window, opened it, and something grabbed me. I tried to get away, but it held my shoulders. Whatever it used to hold me dug into me. See, it cut deep and wouldn't let go."

Melinie slid her shirt off one of her shoulders, revealing a nasty cut with three distinct marks. "I think this came from its claws," she said.

"I think you're right," said Caleb. "The three marks could definitely be from claw marks."

"Is that where the blood came from?" asked Rachelle.

Melinie looked at her shirt; there was dried blood on it. "Yeah, I guess so. I hadn't noticed it until now."

With the stress of everything going on, she guessed her adrenaline had been so high that she hadn't even noticed the blood or pain from the creature's claws digging into her skin, but now she could, and it was hurting quite severely. "I never saw its face because it had me facing down. All I could see was the ground, then the tops of the trees, and pretty much nothing but darkness. I was so scared that it was going to drop me. Between the fear of being dropped and the fear of it taking me, I must have passed out because all I remember after that was struggling to get out of the ground where you guys found me."

"How did you get under the ground?" asked Rachelle.

"I have no idea. I don't know if it buried me or what."

"It buried you, Melinie! That's how I got the idea to start digging. There was fresh dirt where we pulled you out. Like when you go to a new gravesite and can tell someone was just put in the ground. When I saw it, I took a shot that you might be under the ground. I knew it was a total Hail Mary pass, but it was the right choice and the only thing I could think of at the time."

"Thank you so much, Caleb! I don't think I'd be alive if you hadn't done that!"

"You're welcome, sis!"

"Why do you think it buried you?" asked Rachelle.

Seeing clearly that she was struggling with this conversation, Caleb caught Rachelle's attention with a look, then motioned in Melinie's direction. Rachelle nodded, understanding that he was hinting that they needed to stop asking questions for now. In unison, they went over to her and wrapped their arms tightly around her to provide as much comfort to their sister as possible.

"Thank you, guys; I needed that!"

"We're here for you, sis."

"I know. Thank you!" Melinie said.

"What day is it?" asked Rachelle.

"It's Sunday, I think," said Melinie.

"Hey, wasn't Dad's friend Jay supposed to come and check on us sometime this weekend?" asked Rachelle.

"Yeah, he was!" Caleb said with an excited tone. "Hopefully, he'll come today before it gets dark and get us out of here."

"Hopefully!" Rachelle responded. "Do you think he'll believe us?"

"Would you?" asked Melinie.

"Nah, probably not. But either way, we must convince him to take us somewhere safe. Do you guys agree?"

Caleb and Melinie nodded in agreement. The three siblings agreed to wait it out in the basement until Jay arrived to rescue them.

A few hours passed, and there was no sign of Mark's friend Jay. "I don't think he's coming, and it's getting late," said Rachelle.

"I know. He should have been here by now," said Melinie.

"Do you think the creature took him too and that it was him in that car?" asked Caleb.

"Who else could it be? There's no way that Dad would have asked someone to check on us if he wasn't certain that he'd keep his word," said Rachelle.

"So, what now?" asked Caleb.

"Honestly, I have no flippin' idea," said Melinie.

"Should we just stay here until Mom and Dad get home, or what?" asked Rachelle. None of them responded because they had no idea what to do or how to respond.

They waited and waited; no one came, not even their parents. As evening settled in, the basement grew dark, and the sun began to set.

"Guys, the sun is going down. Should we turn on the basement lights before it gets too dark?" Rachelle asked.

"I don't think we should," Melinie responded.

"Yeah, I agree. That might make the creature aware of where we are. Let's keep them off and stay under the stairs until morning," Caleb added.

"Well, I guess we're stuck here for another night," said Rachelle.

"Guess so," said Melinie. Huddled under the basement stairs, they sat quietly, struggling to see the basement as it grew darker every minute.

"What's that?" Rachelle asked in a whisper.

Turning their heads to the far end of the basement, they saw a bright, red light shrouding the basement windows. "Oh, my God, it's here!" cried Melinie.

Caleb covered her mouth. "Shhh, it might hear you."

Melinie quieted, but her breathing intensified. He removed his hand from her mouth, and she remained quiet while keeping her eyes glued to the red light. They hoped that if they waited it out without making a sound, the creature would move on. They kept their eyes fixed in the window's direction for what felt like hours, and the light remained.

The darkness they thought would hide them from being seen by the creature faded quickly as light lit up the basement. "Is that fog?" Melinie asked, her voice trembling.

"Yes, I think so!" Caleb responded.

"I think one of the windows is broken!" Rachelle added. The fog began seeping inside from a small, marble-sized hole in the window.

"Does that mean the monster can get in, too?" asked Rachelle.

"I'm guessing we're not safe down here after all!" said Melinie.

"The light is still outside, so maybe only the fog can get inside," Rachelle said. They huddled closer together, hoping and praying Rachelle was indeed correct.

The fog began filling the basement space quickly, moving closer to them. As it began to encroach on their hiding place, Melinie heard a voice whispering her name. "Melinie!" it whispered.

At first, she thought it was her brother and whispered, "What, Caleb?"

"Huh?" he said.

"Didn't you say my name?" she asked.

"No, I didn't," he responded.

"You didn't whisper my name?" she asked in a shaky voice.

"No, sis, I didn't."

"Melinie!" the voice whispered again.

"Did you hear that?" she asked.

"Hear what?" Rachelle responded.

"I keep hearing my name being whispered," she said with a look of horror. They both said no at the same time. "Oh my God, it's in here!" Melinie screamed. "We have to leave!"

Fearing for her life, Melinie jumped out from under the stairs and zoomed up them in a full sprint. "Stop!" screamed Caleb as he ran after her.

Not looking back, she continued up the stairs without paying attention to her brother's plea. Concerned that the monster might come, Caleb ran up the stairs after her. "Come on, Rachelle, let's go!" he shouted.

However, Rachelle was too scared to move and remained under the stairs. A little quicker than his sister, Caleb caught up to Melinie. Grabbing her arm, he stopped her in her tracks. "Where are you going, Mel?"

"I have to leave here!" she screamed.

"We can't; it's still out there!" he shouted.

"No, it's in here now!" she yelled back.

"If it's in here, why didn't it grab us? All you heard was a voice. Maybe it speaks through the fog but can't come in," he said.

"It's in here in the house, Caleb. I know it's in here," she kept repeating.

"No, it's not! Look, we're safe. Nothing has come after us. Nothing is up here with us, not even the fog!" he said as he pointed around the room. "Look, sis, we're safe. We're safe!" He tried to calm her down.

Melinie looked around the room, then down the hallway; nothing was in the house. He grabbed her hands and led her to the couch. "Sit down, sis," he said. "It's OK; you're safe."

"You just don't understand," she said. "It didn't take *you*. You weren't buried under the ground. You don't understand what I went through." She started crying.

"I know, but I'm here with you," he said. "We are safe. I think it wants us to go outside. We must stay inside. I think it's playing head games to lure us outside, and we can't do that."

Melinie looked at him, then back around the room once more. Seeing that there wasn't anything in the house to cause alarm and that the voice was gone, she said, "Maybe you're right. OK, I'll stay inside. I don't hear the voice anymore, so maybe it is trying to get me outside so it can retake me. Thank you!" She began to calm down. "Wait, where is Rachelle?" She stared wide-eyed at Caleb.

"Crap, she's still down there!" he responded. He ran back toward the basement stairs. "Wait, where is the door?"

The door leading to the basement was gone.

Still sitting under the basement stairs, Rachelle couldn't believe her brother and sister had just left her there. She wanted to follow them up the stairs, but her legs were frozen. She could still see the red light. And now the fog surrounded her.

What if it's in here with me? Can it see me? Can it hear me breathing? Her mind raced with questions. "What do I do?" she asked herself. Trying to keep as still as possible, she kept looking around the room without moving her head. Maybe it wouldn't see her if it didn't see any movement.

"What was that?" she said to herself. From the corner of her eye, she thought she saw something moving through the fog. Scared out of her mind, she held her breath, trying not to make a sound. Keeping her head still but her eyes active, she constantly looked around the room for anything moving there.

After holding her breath as long as possible, she blew out with a louder-than-intended exhale. She quickly covered her mouth. However, something now knew she was there.

Just a few feet away from her came a deep growl. When she jumped up to escape it, the top of her head hit the beam of the stairway directly above her. "Ouch!" she unintentionally shouted. "Oh no! It sees me!"

She was right, and the creature knew precisely where she was.

She could see the creature moving in her direction. Not able to move in any direction without it catching her, she braced herself against the basement wall. Then like treading through water, she began kicking hard and fast to keep it away from her. While doing this, she accidentally kicked what she thought was a wall and heard something hit the floor. Undeterred, she just kept kicking. Even though she typically ran several miles daily for school sports, she could feel her legs starting to give out. Completely exhausted, she stopped momentarily to get enough wind to kick again.

However, her body was so worn out that she couldn't find the strength to keep it up. *I can't do this anymore!* she thought. She waited for it to attack her, but nothing happened. *Why isn't it attacking me? I don't hear its growls anymore. Where did it go?* Confused, she scanned the room for any sign of the creature.

Then, like a tiger leaping to attack its prey, the monster jumped out of the fog, stopping just short of her feet. Suddenly, it let out an unexpected scream, shattering the basement windows. Rachelle covered her face with her arms to protect herself from the creature, but to her surprise and relief, it didn't attack. It just stood there in front of her. It was breathing heavily and seemed afraid.

Why isn't it attacking me? she wondered. She looked at the creature. It appeared to be looking down at something; the monster screamed again, then quickly flew out of one of the broken windows, taking the fog with it.

Completely stunned, Rachelle slowly picked herself up from the basement floor and leaned against the wall. "What happened?" she asked herself. "What made it leave?"

Now that the fog was gone and the creature had left, she found the courage to stand up and leave the basement as quickly as possible. As she went to the stairs, she noticed a book lying in the middle of the floor.

Is that what I kicked? she wondered.

Rachelle walked over to the book and picked it up. *What is this? It looks old! I better take it with me!* Not wanting to be in the basement any longer, she ran up the stairs with the book.

CHAPTER 5

HURRY HOME, BETH

Lying face down on the living room floor, Beth began to stir; she was waking up. "When did I fall asleep?" she asked herself. Struggling to see clearly, she rubbed her eyes to help remove the blurriness. As everything began to focus, she scanned the room before standing to her feet. Everything seemed quiet. There was no sign of the creature.

Standing, she made her way to the front door, which was wide open. Her legs felt weak and shaky. As she reached the door, Beth cautiously looked outside; there was no fog or sign of what had taken Zack and her little brother.

Doing her best to focus, she looked farther down the driveway. "Zack's car is still there," she said. Not wanting to be there anymore, she decided to take Zack's car and drive to the house. *I have to get to my brother and sisters*, she thought. Before heading to the car, she took another good look each way to ensure it was clear. With her legs still not secure under her, she awkwardly power walked to the car, stepping inside the driver's seat.

"Where are the keys? Dang it!" she yelled. "That's right; I remember seeing Zack place them on the key rack hanging in the kitchen. Well, I guess I'm heading back to the house," Knowing she had no choice but not wanting to get out of the car, Beth sat there for a few minutes, running scenarios in her head before deciding what to do.

Beth how grown up watching scary movies with her dad. This

situation caused flashbacks of how each of those movies had played out. *Either it's safe to get the keys, or the monster is going to catch me outside*, she thought. Struggling with her thoughts, she finally decided she had only two options: either run to the house to get the keys or forget the keys and walk home. Neither option gave her any peace of mind.

"Walking isn't a viable option because I have no idea how far it is. So, retrieving the keys it is. If it wants me, it will have to catch me. Why, oh why, didn't I run track at school?" she questioned. "Come on, legs, don't fail me now!"

Without a second thought to deter her, she immediately hit a full sprint speed after stepping outside the car. Running more quickly than she thought she could, she slipped through the front door, slammed it closed behind her, and made a beeline straight to the kitchen.

Not taking a second to catch her breath, Beth grabbed the keys and went straight out the back door. Maybe going out the back would throw the creature off and give her additional time to get ahead of it, she thought. Making it back to Zack's car in record time, Beth stepped inside and locked the car door, then placed the keys in the ignition. Unlike the scary movies she watched, the car started on the first try, and off she went.

"I can't believe it!" she said. "Zack has a GPS in his car." She squealed with glee. "I guess it makes sense with the horrible signal out here, but I can't believe it!" After plugging in the address of her parents' home, she followed the navigator's voice, which told her which way to go. "I'm only five minutes away. I'll be home in no time." Checking her mirrors often, she saw nothing following her, and there wasn't any fog to be concerned about. For once, everything seemed to be OK.

Not paying attention to the speed limit, she had the car racing at ninety-five miles per hour. The five-minute trip took less than three minutes. "There it is!" she yelled. Her parents' driveway was just ahead. "I can't wait to see my brother and sisters!"

When she decided to glance in the rearview mirror one last time, her feelings of relief turned to dread. The same fog surrounding Zack's house rapidly rolled up behind her. Beth stomped on the gas pedal to ensure the fog didn't catch up to her.

She wasn't willing to slow down; the car slid sideways into the driveway, taking out the mailbox. Determined to keep the pedal to the floor, she and the car barreled toward the house. She switched her foot from the gas to the brakes but not soon enough. The vehicle collided with the front porch, causing the airbag to explode.

Dazed by the crash's impact, Beth fell to the ground when she opened the door to get out. Knowing the fog was approaching the home, she stumbled up the front porch steps, screaming to be let inside while pounding on the door. "Let me in!" she shouted.

Hearing her sister screaming, Melinie ran to the door and let her in. After entering the house, Beth quickly slammed the door, locking it tight. Because of the damage done to the door by the creature earlier, she struggled to close it properly since it wouldn't align with the deadbolt. After working with it, she finally got the deadbolt slid over. Just as it latched, there was a loud banging on the door. Startled, Beth jumped away from the door.

Keeping her eyes glued to the door, Beth walked backward toward her brother and sisters. Refusing to take her eyes off the door, Beth grabbed each of their hands as if to say, *I'm here; it'll be all right!* as she squeezed them firmly. They all stood there, holding each other's hands tightly and waiting to see what would happen next.

Also, while racing back home, Mark couldn't get the voice he had heard over the phone out of his head. It had sounded human, but it must have been something else entirely with what it could do through the phone. *"Say my name!" I've heard that before,* he thought. Mark was so scared for his children. He knew that whatever was on the other line was pure evil and that his children were in danger.

Mark and Amber were eight hours away from home. He felt so helpless. *I was so stupid to leave them!* he thought. *I thought they would be safe, and that Jay would watch over them. What happened to Jay? Why is this happening?* He fought hard to keep his wits about him. He did his best to keep himself composed for his wife, who was so emotionally shaken. They were both concerned about the well-being of their kids and if he didn't keep it together, he would only worsen the situation.

The road was covered with fog, making it impossible to see anything. Several times he nearly ran off the road because the fog was so thick. The speed limit was fifty-five, but the best he could do was around thirty-five miles per hour. *At this rate, it will take ten hours or more to get to them,* he thought. *I must find a way to get there faster. Come on, fog, clear up. I must get to my kids!*

"'Say my name!' 'Say my name!' Where have I heard that? I know I've heard that before," Mark whispered.

"What?" said Amber.

Mark didn't realize he had spoken loudly enough for Amber to hear him. "Oh, nothing, Amber."

"No!" said Amber. "What did you hear before?" She looked at him.

"I-I-I think I've heard that phrase before."

"What phrase?" Amber asked.

"The voice said, 'Say my name!'"

"Yeah? I heard it too. What does it mean, Mark? Have you heard it before?" Amber asked.

"I think so. I can't remember where, but it seems familiar to me somehow."

"Mark, if you know what it means, you must remember," Amber said sternly.

"I know! I'm trying!" Mark said, irritated. "Just let me think for a minute, OK, Amber?" He began to whisper the phrase over and over. "'Say my name!' 'Say my name!'"

Like a movie playing in his head, he suddenly remembered where he had heard the phrase. "I remember, Amber!"

"Remember what, Mark?"

"I remember why that phrase is so familiar to me. It's from a child-hood memory."

"Where did you hear it before, Mark?"

"I remember it so clearly now! I think I had to be five or six years old at the time. My parents had a group of people over to the house. They were acting as if something was wrong. My dad took me to the bedroom, ordering me to stay in my room until they came and got me, but I didn't listen; I was too curious. When I heard them walking down the steps after leaving my room, I stepped into the hall to hear what was happening. After a few minutes, someone shouted, 'Whatever happens, don't say his name!' Then there was this awful scream."

"Scared to death, I ran straight back to my room, covering my head with the covers until they came in to get me. I never asked them what had happened, even to this day. After a while, I just quit thinking about it or blocked it from my memory. But, whatever occurred, it must have been rough because that was the only time, I remember seeing my dad look afraid."

"Mark, why would you move us to this god-awful town knowing about this?"

"I swear I didn't know! I knew it somewhere in my subconscious, but it was like it had been erased from my memory until now. Please believe me! If I had remembered it, there's no way I would've moved our family to the farm."

"I'm sorry for getting upset with you, Mark. I'm just so worried about the kids. I believe you. Do you think that event has anything to do with what is happening with our kids right now?" Amber asked.

"Not sure, but we need to get to them as quickly as possible, but with this fog being so thick, it will take a long while."

"Please try to drive faster, Mark!"

"I'm trying, Amber. I'm trying!"

Several hours later, Mark and Amber finally arrived in their town and were just a few miles from their house.

"Just ten more minutes, and we'll be there!" Mark said.

"What if something happened to them?" Amber asked in a very worrisome tone.

"We can't think that way!" Mark responded.

"Yeah, but what if they aren't even there?" Amber asked.

"Amber! They will be OK! We will see them soon. Our children are fine!" He was trying to reassure Amber while denying he had the same fears.

Salt Hills was a tiny town. It was one of those towns people would call a blink-once-and-you'll-miss-it kind of place. It had a grocery store that also doubled as the only gas station within twenty miles. Other than that, there were a couple of churches and a post office, and that was just about it.

As they stopped at the four-way stop before getting on the curvy state route that took them to their home, all the lights suddenly went out in their little community. Being a little town, there weren't many lights in the first place, making stargazing easy. However, this darkness carried a strange, ominous feeling.

Mark pushed hard on the gas pedal; the car stalled. "Mark, did it die?" Amber asked.

"Yes!" Mark responded. Putting the car in park, Mark turned the ignition key to get the car started again; the engine refused to turn over. He tried again. Nothing. Mark slammed his fists on the steering wheel and yelled a few choice profanities at the car.

"I have to get out to look under the hood," Mark grumbled.

"No! Don't get out of the car, Mark!" Amber pleaded.

"I have to!" Refusing to listen to his wife's appeal, Mark pulled the hood release, then stepped out of the car. Walking around the front of the vehicle, he lifted the hood to see if he could figure out why the car had stalled.

Amber tried her best to keep an eye on Mark but struggled to see anything in such foggy conditions with no lights to help her. *How will he fix the car with no lights?* she wondered. *If only we still had our phones, we could use their light.* "Mark, can you see to fix it?"

Mark didn't answer.

"Mark? Honey, are you OK? Please answer me!"

Still, Mark didn't respond.

"Honey, did you hear me?" she asked loudly.

Still, there was no answer.

"Mark! Answer me!" she yelled.

Still no response from him.

Against her better judgment, Amber opened the door to check on Mark. Shaking uncontrollably, she made her way to the front of the car.

There was Mark. He appeared to be bent over, looking at the engine. "Mark is everything OK?" she asked. Mark didn't answer. He didn't seem to be moving either.

Walking a little closer, Amber reached out to touch his shoulder. Mark?" As her hand touched him, she saw a strange red light within the fog and heard a deep, growling sound. Launching herself backward from fright, she fell to the ground on her back.

Looking up, she watched Mark rise slowly into the air. Mark's eyes caught her gaze, but he appeared incapacitated; his body leaned over as if his muscles had utterly given out on him.

"Mark!" she yelled.

His mouth quivered as if he were trying to respond, but no words came out. Not seeing anything holding him up, Amber crawled toward him, grabbing his leg to pull him down, screaming, "Mark, no!"

Suddenly, a large, winged creature stepped out of the fog, appearing to be holding Mark with claw-like hands. It easily stood over eight feet tall. Mark stood just shy of six feet and one inch, but the winged creature towered over him, even with Mark hovering above the ground.

Stepping forward toward her with Mark dangling in its clutches, the creature looked at Amber. With it facing her, she could see humanlike features on its face, but somehow this was no human. Its two normal eyes remained fixed on her, but it also had a large, glowing red eye in its chest area. "Say my name!" it shouted.

Amber knew this was what she and her husband had heard on the phone. "Say my name!" it repeated.

"I don't know your name!" Amber responded.

Visibly upset, the creature screamed at her, "*Say my name!*"

Amber didn't know the creature's name, but even if she did, she remembered one thing from the story Mark had told her: "Whatever happens, don't say its name!" That's what Mark had heard the people say about this creature those many years ago. She was convinced that this was whom they had been referring to all those years ago.

"I don't know your name. Now let him go!" she shouted.

This response made the creature angry. Knocking her across the road, it let out a horrific scream before extending its wings and disappearing into the night with Mark clutched in its massive wings.

Severely injured but determined to fight through the pain, Amber ran down the dark road, yelling Mark's name, but there was no sign of him or the creature that had taken him. They were gone; she was alone.

Amber limped back to the car, leaving a trail of blood from the wounds on her legs from when the creature had knocked her across the road. She stepped inside and tried to start the car; it came alive. Shoving it into drive, she nearly lost control of the vehicle as she took off like a crazed maniac, desperate to get home.

"This is too much to take! My family is gone!" she yelled. "I'm not letting this happen. Whatever it takes, I will get them back. I'll find a way to move heaven and hell if necessary." She pointed toward the sky.

"There's the house!" said Amber. Before entering the driveway, a thought came to her mind. *What if it's there with them? If it sees me, will it harm the kids?* she wondered. Deciding that she needed to be stealthy, she pulled the car off to the side of the road. Then, turning off the car, Amber quietly exited the vehicle.

I'll head through the woods so it can't see me, she thought. *The lights are on. That is a good sign.* Using the trees as cover, she made her way toward the house. As she drew closer, she heard something moving through the grass behind her.

Amber spun around to see what it was. When she took a long look to scan the area, the sound stopped; nothing was moving. *Hopefully, that was just a normal little animal,* she thought.

Continuing to listen for any new movement, she got back on course toward the house. Reaching the barn, she heard something behind her again. This time when she looked, there was a glowing red light on one of the trees. *Crap, it's out here with me!* she thought as she lay in the tall grass to hide from it.

Looking through the grass, she could tell it was moving through it but not in her general direction. *Maybe it hasn't seen me*, she thought. Counting on that being the case, she crawled toward the house military style, ensuring to stay below the height of the grass.

Nearly reaching the house's backyard, she heard a whooshing sound above her. *What was that?* she wondered. Lifting her eyes to the sky, she saw nothing fly overhead. "Don't stop now; you're almost there, girl!" she told herself.

Whoosh!

There it was again. Taking a quick look to see where the red light was, she couldn't locate it anywhere. *Is it flying above me?* she wondered. Starting to panic, she turned back toward the house to go for it.

"No!" She stopped dead in her tracks.

Fog surrounded the house. Deciding her life was in danger either way, she took off running.

When she got within a few feet of the back door, her feet sank into the mud. Struggling to free herself, a hand popped up from the ground and grabbed her legs. She tried to pry it off, but it only tightened its grip. As she squirmed to get free, the hand began pulling her farther into the mud. Quickly, she found herself chest deep in the sinking ground.

"There are the kids!" she cried. She saw them through the window. Screaming to them, she realized her voice made no sound.

Why can't they hear me? Why can't I scream? she wondered. She felt something else moving against her legs.

An arm exploded through the mud behind her body. Covering the top of her head, it wrapped its long finger-like talons over her face, pushing her down into the earth. She screamed and caught one last glimpse of her children before she was dragged entirely under the ground.

CHAPTER 6

POSSESSED

The knocking continued, but they wouldn't open the door. "Open the door!" the creature shouted.

"What do we do, Beth?" asked Caleb. Beth didn't know how to respond. "Beth?"

"I don't know! Is it safe here? Can it get in?"

"It hasn't yet been upstairs, but we think it might have come inside the basement where Rachelle is!"

"She's downstairs?" asked Beth. Caleb and Melinie brought Beth up to speed on what had happened to Rachelle. "Why did you leave her down there?"

"It was an accident! We thought she was right behind us, and now we don't know how to get her out!" said Melinie. "What are we going to do? How are we going to get to Rachelle?"

"I don't know, sis!" said Beth.

"How can the door disappear?" asked Caleb.

Wanting to confirm their story, Beth went to where the basement door was supposed to be. There was an outline of a door but no actual door. She felt all around, looking for a way in. "There's nothing here!" she screamed while banging on the wall. "This can't be happening!"

Melinie and Caleb ran over to her. "There has to be a way in!" Melinie shouted.

"Wait. What about the basement windows?" asked Caleb. "One

window is broken, so we can probably break it the rest of the way and get to her that way."

The thought of going outside was more than Melinie could handle. "I can't go out there!" she said. "What if it's out there, waiting for us? I-I-I just can't …"

Before Melinie could finish, her eyes rolled back in her head, and she stood there, motionless.

"Sis, are you OK?" Beth asked.

She still wasn't moving.

Caleb noticed she was trying to whisper something. Moving toward her, he asked nervously, "Mel, are you OK?"

While she was still whispering something, Melinie's body lifted off the floor a few inches like she was floating and moved toward him. "Mel?" Caleb shouted as he stumbled backward.

Melinie continued moving in his direction, whispering something he couldn't hear or understand.

"Caleb, get away from her!" Beth shouted.

Caleb ran toward Beth to get away from Melinie. Beth grabbed his hands, and they ran to the bathroom to escape her. Once inside, they locked the door and leaned hard against it to keep her from getting inside.

"Let me in!" Melinie shouted.

Beth and Caleb continued pushing hard against the door to keep her out. "Let me in!" Melinie shouted again. However, this wasn't their sister's voice; it was deep and horrible sounding.

"Mel! Stop! Let her go!" Beth shouted through the door.

"Let me in!" the voice called back at them.

"Let her go!"

"Why are you saying, 'Let her go,' Beth?"

"That's not Melinie, Caleb!"

"What do you mean?"

"I'll tell you later!"

"What do you want?" Beth cried.

"Say my name!" the voice shouted. Beth and Caleb looked at each other. "Say my name!" the voice called again.

"OK, what's your name? We'll say it," Beth shouted. "Just stop!"

Mel began knocking on the door. Caleb was tempted to say, "Who is it?" But he stopped himself; now wasn't the time to be cute.

"Say my name!" This time the words came with a whisper and sounded like Melinie.

"What is she doing? That's Melinie's voice. Are you sure it's not her, Beth?"

"It's not her, Caleb! It's trying to make us take our guard down so we will open the door."

"Beth, why won't you open the door?" Melinie asked.

"Because you're not Melinie. Now, let her go!" Beth demanded.

Melinie screamed, and something thudded outside the door.

"Did she leave, Beth?" Caleb whispered.

"Mel?" Beth whispered.

"Beth?" Mel said quietly.

"Mel, is that you?" Beth asked.

"Yes, it's me. What's going on?"

"Step away from the door, Caleb," Beth said. Beth opened the door to find Melinie lying on the floor before the bathroom door. Cautiously, Beth went over to her. "Mel is that you?" she asked.

"What do you mean?" she asked. "Of course, it's me. Can you help me up?" Melinie asked Beth.

Beth put her hands under her shoulders and helped Melinie from the floor. "What happened?" Melinie asked Beth.

"I think something just possessed you," said Beth.

"What do you mean?" asked Melinie.

"Your eyes rolled in the back of your head, and you were floating in the air. Then your voice changed; it wasn't you, sis!"

"I don't believe you!"

"Tell her, Caleb!"

"Beth is telling the truth, Mel. Do you remember anything?"

"I remember you talking about going outside to see if we could get

Rachelle out from the basement window and then waking up on the floor. Wait! I remember hearing a voice say my name, and everything went black."

"I think that whatever that thing is outside got inside you somehow, Mel," Caleb said.

"What? It was inside me?" she asked.

"I think so," Caleb said.

"I don't know what happened, but obviously, it's able to get to you, Mel," said Beth. "We have to get you out of here before something terrible happens."

"I agree!" Melinie said.

As they were talking, they heard a door slam. "What was that?" asked Caleb.

"It sounded like it came from the hallway. We need to check it out!" said Beth. Worried that the creature had made its way inside, they grabbed whatever defense tool they could find before checking out what had caused the sound.

Caleb grabbed a broom; the other two grabbed knives from the kitchen. Getting in their best defensive positions, they slowly walked through the living room and toward the hallway. Caleb led the charge and raised the broom over his head, ready to hit the creature with the handle when it showed its face. He was armed and ready to take it head-on when Rachelle suddenly met him face-to-face as she appeared from around the corner.

Not knowing it was her at first, he swung the broom, hitting the wall and barely missing her head. "Oh, my God, Rachelle!" he yelled.

"What the … you almost killed me, Caleb!"

"I'm so sorry, Rachelle! I thought you were the creature!"

"Well, I'm not, so you can put down the broom."

"Oh, yeah!" he said, laughing. "Are you OK?"

"Yes, I'm fine. No thanks to you and Mel leaving me in the basement alone!" said Rachelle.

Hearing Rachelle's voice, Melinie ran over to her. "Are you OK?" Melinie asked as she gave Rachelle a huge hug.

"Yeah, but like I said, no thanks to you both!"

"We're so sorry! We thought you were right behind us," said Melinie.

"Well, I wasn't!"

Rachelle looked past them to find Beth staring at her with tears running down her cheeks. Beth ran over to her. "I missed you so much! I thought you had been taken or worse. I'm so glad to see you!" Beth said as she gave her a huge bear hug.

"Where were you?" asked Caleb.

"I was in the basement," Rachelle said.

Caleb and Melinie went on to tell Rachelle about how the basement door had just disappeared. "Well, it's there now because that's how I got out of the basement," she said.

"How is that possible?" asked Caleb.

"I have no idea, but I have something to tell you guys!" Rachelle went on to share with them what had happened downstairs. She then showed them the book.

"The monster was scared of this?" Caleb asked Rachelle.

"I'm guessing so because when it got close to it, it flew out the window, screaming."

Beth grabbed the book from Rachelle's hands. She tried to open it, but it was sealed tight. "Yeah, I already tried that, but it won't open," Rachelle said.

"Look! It has a seal or something on it," said Melinie.

"Grab a butter knife," Beth told Caleb. He grabbed the knife and gave it to Beth. Beth pried and pried, but the book wouldn't open. Putting down the knife, Beth began inspecting the book. "Man, it's dusty! It must have been down there a while." Wiping the dust off, she noticed a strange symbol with an inscription that said, "Sealed with blood. Keep his name unspoken." Turning the book over, she saw names written on the back.

"Guys, look at this!" she said to her siblings. "That's Grandpa and Grandma's names. It has their names written on it."

Caleb grabbed the book from Beth's hands. "It does!" he exclaimed. "Why are their names on here?"

Beth grabbed the book back and said, "I don't know, but clearly, this is important! They must know what this creature is. We've got to find a way to talk to them."

"Have you guys tried to leave?" Beth asked.

"Just once," said Melinie. "This thick fog rolls in, and then—"

"Yeah, I know. Then the creature comes after you. It happened to me too," said Beth. She thought momentarily, then asked, "Rachelle, where was this book?"

"Under the basement stairs."

"Then let's go down there. Maybe there's something down there that will help us," Beth said.

"What if the door disappears again and we can't get back up?" asked Caleb.

"Then we go with your plan of using the window," said Beth.

"Sorry, Melinie!"

"Yeah, whatever!" Melinie responded.

"Lead the way, Rachelle," said Beth.

Rachelle led them to where she had been when she found the book. "Here is where I was. It must've fallen from somewhere under the stairs."

"Caleb, you keep watch while we start looking," Beth told Caleb. He agreed. As he kept watch, the other three began searching under the stairs.

"Hey, I found something!" Melinie shouted. Beth, Rachelle, and Caleb walked over to Melinie. "It's the same symbol that's on the book," she told them.

"It is!" said Rachelle. They all looked at the symbol that Melinie found underneath the top stair. It was the same symbol, but it was covered with something red.

"Is that paint?" Melinie asked.

At that moment, Beth recalled what the book had said. "I think it is blood," she said. "Just like it says on the front cover of the book. 'Sealed with blood. Keep his name unspoken.'"

"What blood? Whose blood?" asked Rachelle.

"I'm thinking those whose names are written on the back of the book. Yeah, and this house used to be our grandparents' place, right?" asked Caleb.

"Yes, it did," Melinie responded.

"So, if that's blood, are you saying Grandpa and Grandma put blood on this symbol?" Rachelle asked.

"It's the only thing that makes sense," said Beth.

"Makes sense? How does any of this make sense? Were our grandparents involved in some blood cult or something?" Rachelle asked.

"I can't see them being involved in something like that, but it does appear that they faced this thing way back when, and they know what it takes to get rid of it. So, we must find a way out of here and head to their house," Beth added.

"We can't leave! We've tried. It won't let us," said Rachelle.

"Rachelle, we don't have a choice. While you were downstairs, something happened to Melinie," said Beth. She took a few minutes to explain what had happened and how important it was to get away before it happened again.

"Melinie, are you OK now?" Rachelle asked.

"I think so. I don't remember anything. I guess it took me over completely. I am scared it might do it again, though, so I agree that we must find a way to escape as soon as possible."

"All right, I'm all ears. Who has an idea?" asked Rachelle.

"Beth, whose car is that?" asked Caleb.

"That's a long story!" said Beth.

"Well, is it drivable?" Caleb asked.

"Only one way to find out," Beth said as she shrugged. "But we'll have to find a way to get it off the porch first. I couldn't hit the brakes in time when I was trying to get here, and I slammed into the porch, making the front of the car jump up onto the porch!"

"Nice driving, sis!" Caleb said.

Beth rolled her eyes.

"Leave it to me. I'll get it off the porch; I hope it's drivable when I do," Caleb responded.

"Me too!" said Beth.

"You guys ready to leave?" Caleb asked with a smirk.

"What choice do we have?" asked Melinie.

"All right, pack your stuff; we're leaving," Caleb said.

"What if the creature is out there?" asked Melinie.

"We must take that chance! Rachelle, you keep watch while I head outside. The rest of you, pack up some essentials into some backpacks; we're getting out of here!"

CHAPTER 7

JOE AND MARY

"Have you talked to Mark today?" Mary asked her husband, Joe.

"Nope! It's been a couple of days; why?"

"I've been trying to reach them all day, but they're not answering."

"Cell service is nonexistent at the farm, so I'm not surprised!" said Joe.

"They're not at the farm; they went out of town to that little resort up north, remember?"

"That's right!" said Joe. "Have you tried Amber's phone?"

"Yep! Her phone doesn't even ring. What if something is wrong, Joe?"

"I'm sure it's fine, sweetheart. Try again in a couple of hours, and if you don't get through, we'll drive up to the house to check on them, OK?"

"OK, Joe, but if they don't answer, we'll drive there tonight!" Mary demanded.

"Of course, Mary. I'm on the same page with you."

Joe and Mary had lived most of their married lives at the farm where her son, Mark, and his family were now living. Yes, they missed country life, but now that they were older, they appreciated not having to deal with the farm and all the work that came along with it. Joe was fortunate enough to enjoy a well-funded pension. So, instead of selling the home, they decided to deed it to Mark and move into the city.

This was the home where they had raised their three kids. Mark was their youngest; then there were his two older sisters, Valerie and Brooke.

Brooke was the oldest, and Valerie was the middle child. Neither had been interested in the farm, but Mark had been thrilled to take it.

Two hours later …

"Hon, Mark's still not answering," Mary said with a concerned tone.

"OK, let's go!" said Joe. He was sure everything was OK, but he knew better than to discount his wife's concerns. "At least leave a voice mail, letting them know we're coming. Maybe they're at the pool and will get back to us when they see the voice mail."

"I would if it let me. It doesn't go to voice mail. It just keeps ringing; that's why I'm concerned."

"Oh, that is a little strange," said Joe.

"Joe, do you think—"

"No, don't even think that. It's been over forty years. There's no way it's that. Unless …"

"Unless what, Joe?" Mary asked.

"Unless one of the symbols has been damaged somehow."

"We must check to see if the symbols remain intact, Joe!" Mary said with a shaky voice.

"We will! Let's get to Mark and his family first, though."

Caleb slowly ventured outside to see if the coast was clear. "Guys, you won't believe this!" he shouted.

"What is it?" asked Beth.

"Come and look!"

Beth went to the door and looked outside. "The fog is gone!" said Beth.

"I know! I can't believe it!"

"Well, let's not wait for it to come back!"

"I agree!" Beth told the other two girls to get the backpacks and head outside. "The fog is gone, so let's get the car off the porch and get out of here!"

Melinie and Rachelle nodded, retrieved the backpacks, and tossed them in the car.

"Beth, get in the car and try to back off the porch while I push!"

"Got it!"

"OK, Beth, are you ready?"

"Ready!" With Caleb pushing on the front of the car, Beth put it in reverse and gave it some gas. "It's not working!" she yelled back.

"Mel! Rachelle! Come help me!" Caleb shouted. "We're going to rock the car back and forth to see if we can get the front wheels off the porch while Beth hits the gas, OK?"

"Ok!" they said.

"OK, hit it, sis!" Caleb said to Beth. With Beth hitting the gas and Caleb, Melinie, and Rachelle pushing the car, they tried their best to get it off the porch.

"I think it's starting to move!" Beth yelled. "Keep pushing, guys!"

"What the—? Beth, get out of the car!" yelled Melinie.

Beth looked out the rearview mirror. She saw the creature flying toward them, carrying the fog along with it.

"Get out of the car!" Melinie screamed again at Beth.

"I'm trying, but the door won't open!" she cried.

"Climb out the window!" Caleb yelled.

Beth rolled down the window and began crawling out.

"She's not moving fast enough!" Rachelle yelled. Caleb ran to the window, grabbed her arms, and yanked her out of the car.

Caleb grabbed his sister. He and Beth joined their sisters as they all ran back inside the house, locking the door behind them. "Let's block the door!" Rachelle yelled.

"Good idea!" shouted Beth. Grabbing the couch, they slid it in front of the door to create an additional line of defense from the creature.

Immediately, Beth ran to the window to see if the creature was outside. "Um, where is the car?" she asked.

"What do you mean?" asked Rachelle.

"It's not there!" she responded.

"It took the car?" Melinie asked. "Great! Now, what are we going to do? What if it takes me over again? What if ..." Melinie collapsed on the floor and started seizing.

"Grab a pillow for her head!" Beth shouted. Rachelle grabbed a pillow and slid it under her head to keep her from injuring herself.

"What do we do?" asked Caleb.

"It's a seizure. We need to stand back and let it run its course. There's nothing else we can do until it's over," said Beth.

"Why is she having a seizure?" asked Caleb.

"It's probably from anxiety," said Beth.

"Do you think it's the creature taking her over?" asked Rachelle.

"No, it's just a seizure. She'll be OK in a few minutes. But she will be too weak to do anything for a while, so our plan to get out of here will have to wait," Beth said.

After filling the car with gas, Joe and Mary headed to the farm. "Do you think the book is still at the house?" asked Mary.

"Let's hope so!" Joe replied.

"What if the kids found it? What if they found a way to open it?" she asked.

"It's sealed, sweetheart. Without the other three, there's no way to open it. Even if they did find it and somehow found a way to open it, nothing would happen without the key," said Joe.

"Should you call Brooke, just in case?" asked Mary.

"Mary! Stop jumping to conclusions!" Joe said, scolding her. "If it turns out that he's been released, then I'll consider calling her, but I'm sure that is not the case, OK?"

"But Joe—"

"No, Mary, we'll wait, OK?"

Extremely frustrated with Joe's insistence, Mary said, "Fine, Joe, we'll wait, but if something happens to those kids, you'll have to carry that weight alone because I warned you."

Joe refused to respond to Mary.

"Joe?"

"I heard you, Mary!" he said.

Mary just stared at Joe for a moment, hoping for a better response from him. When she didn't get one, she leaned back in her seat and said, "Drive faster, Joe!" Joe obliged and stepped on the gas.

"Mel, are you OK?" asked Rachelle.

"My head hurts!" she whimpered. "What happened to me?"

"You had a seizure," answered Beth.

"A seizure? Really?" asked Melinie.

"We tried to protect your head with a pillow, but your seizure was intense, and keeping it under your head was nearly impossible," said Caleb.

"Thank you for trying!" said Melinie. "So, do we try another way of escape?"

"Uh, that's not going to work, sis. The creature is too fast; we wouldn't have a chance," said Caleb.

"So, what now?" asked Rachelle.

"Spend another night here, I guess," said Beth.

"We're never getting out of here!" said Melinie.

"Yes, we will. Somehow, we will make it out," Beth said emphatically.

"I hope you're right, Beth!" Rachelle said.

"Me too!"

"Joe, where is the house?"

Pulling off to the side of the road, Joe looked out Mary's window. "It's not there, Mary!"

Joe quickly exited the car and ran up the hill until he reached an empty lot where a house had once stood. He dropped to his knees, seeing the house no longer. "I can't believe it! It's gone! It's been released! Why did this happen?" He was overwhelmed with a sense of dread.

"Joe!" yelled Mary. "Is there anything left?"

"Nothing at all!" said Joe, shaking his head. "It's all gone, Mary! Even the basement is gone. The symbol is gone. I can't believe this!"

"Joe, get in the car!"

"Mary, you were right! The creature has been released!"

"Joe, get in the car! We must get to the kids!"

"I can't do this again, Mary!"

"Joe, get off your knees! We must go now!"

"I can't do this again!" Joe said, weeping bitterly.

Mary ran up the hill to Joe. "Joe, I know this is a lot to handle right now, but we must think of Mark and his family. Get up, Joe; we must go!

"OK, OK, let's head to the farm," Joe responded.

After leaving the site, Joe said, "Mary, if he's truly been released, there's a chance we won't find them at the farm."

"I know, but we must try anyway, Joe."

"I know, Mary, but I'm not as strong as before, and my blood won't be accepted this time. If they're alive, you know what they must do."

"Let's hope it doesn't come to that, Joe."

"Beth, I have a question," said Caleb.

"Yeah?"

Struggling to get the words out, Caleb asked, "W-w-where is Chase?"

"What do you mean, 'Where is Chase?'" asked Melinie. "He's with Dad and Mom, right, sis?"

Beth looked down and didn't answer.

"Beth?" asked Melinie. Beth remained silent.

"I assumed since he wasn't with you that Dad and Mom must have met you in town and took him with them. Is that what happened?" asked Rachelle.

"He's not with them," Beth said.

"Where is our little brother, Beth?" asked Caleb.

"It's my fault!" Beth said, starting to cry. "It was my job to protect him." Her siblings sat there, just staring at her.

"He's gone?" Melinie asked.

"The creature took him!" said Beth. "It took him, and I couldn't stop it!"

Filled with rage, Caleb picked up a kitchen chair and threw it at the wall. "No!" he shouted. His sisters wanted to try to calm him down, but they were too emotional to do or say anything.

"What happened, Beth?" Melinie asked angrily.

"Melinie, calm down! Beth is hurting! Give her time!" Rachelle said.

"Calm down? Our little brother was taken. How can I calm down? We must find him! What if he's going through what I did? What if he's all alone under the ground or what if ..." Melinie stopped herself and took a breath. "Beth, I'm sorry! I know it's not your fault. I'm just so scared for Chase."

"It's OK!" said Beth. "I can't blame you for being upset. I saw him being taken and ..." Beth couldn't say anything and started bawling. "We have to find him!" she managed to say through her tears.

"We will! We will!" said Rachelle.

Meanwhile, as Joe and Mary made their way to the farm, Joe noticed that the sky had begun to grow dark. "Mary, what time is it?"

"It's four thirty," Mary responded.

"Are we expecting a storm today?" asked Joe.

"I don't think so. Why?"

"Look at the sky; it's too early for the sun to set," said Joe.

"Joe, we need to hurry; that looks like fog."

Joe stopped the car immediately.

"Joe, why are you stopping?"

"Mary, you know what happens if we drive into the fog. We can't go any farther."

"But the kids."

"I know! We will get to them but not this way. We're no good to them if we're taken or worse, Mary!"

As a kid, Joe had spent most of his time in the woods surrounding the farm. If there was one person who could find his way anywhere in this town, it was Joe. "I know another way to get there. But we will have to ditch the car and walk," said Joe.

"Walk?" asked Mary.

"Yeah, it's the only option we got, and it's still a risk."

"OK, Joe, I trust you."

Joe turned the car around and backtracked about a quarter mile before pulling the car off to the side of the road. "Ready, Mary?"

"Does it matter? We must do what we must do."

"OK, sweetheart, grab the flashlight from the trunk and follow me."

Trusting that Joe knew what he was doing, Mary followed him closely as they trekked through the woods.

"Joe, it looks like the fog is staying away from us."

"Thank God!" said Joe. "Look, hold my hand, and don't let go. This area has many sinkholes, and I don't want you to step into one."

Mary grabbed Joe's hand tightly, watching where she was stepping.

"OK, see that tree line?" asked Joe. "We must follow that down to the creek that runs through the farm property," said Joe. "Once we hit the creek, we must follow it to the backside of the farm, OK?"

"OK, Joe. You lead, and I will follow."

Back at the farm, Joe and Mary's grandkids were trying to figure out what to do next. "Look, guys, we're not getting anywhere just sitting here, being all emotional. We need to find a way out," Rachelle said sternly and sarcastically.

"Rachelle, we know this, but how?" asked Caleb.

"Yeah! It's not like we haven't tried!" said Melinie.

"Beth, what do you think we should do?" asked Rachelle.

"Honestly, I have no freaking idea! What's the use? We're not getting out of here, so we might as well just …"

"Beth! Don't even!" Rachelle said. "I know you're hurting and have been through a lot with what happened to Chase and all, but we can't give up. We must keep trying for him, OK?"

"You're right, but it's not just Chase; I lost Zack too!" Beth replied.

"Zack? Who is Zack?" Rachelle asked.

With a deep sigh, Beth gave them the short version of all she had gone through with losing their little brother and then Zack. "Oh my God, sis, I'm so sorry!" said Melinie.

"It's OK. You didn't know, but you had your own nightmare, and I can't imagine what you went through either. Rachelle, you're right. Chase needs us, and maybe there's a chance for Zack too!"

Beth stood up and said, "Let's get them back! We are not going to give up! Thank you, Rachelle, for not letting me fall into despair and reminding me why we need to fight. Chase and Zack are counting on us, and we will not disappoint them."

"I agree, sis, but where do we start?" asked Caleb.

"With the book," Beth responded. "If the creature is afraid of it, we must figure out how to use the book against it. We must figure out how to open it; it's all we have."

Back outside, Joe and Mary made their way to the creek. "OK, now, let's follow the creek up to the property," Joe told Mary. "Mary, if you see the fog or a red light, let me know."

"Why a red light, Joe?"

"That's right, you were in the house and didn't see that. He has a large, red eye in the middle of his chest; it was part of his transformation. When he's hunting in the fog, it shines brightly. He also uses it to draw people to him before they're taken. If you see that, we need to get out of its sight before it shines on us, or we are … well, we need to see it before it sees us."

"Got it, Joe!"

"Ouch!" screamed Mary.

"Mary, what happened?"

"I stepped in a hole and twisted my ankle a little."

"Are you OK? Can you walk?"

"I think so." She took another step and cried out in pain. "Joe, it's bad! I don't think I can walk on it."

"Mary, are you sure? We are so close to the house."

"I can try again, Joe. Ouch! Joe, I can't; I'm sorry! You're going to have to leave me."

"I'm not leaving you, Mary!"

Joe wasn't the strong young man he used to be, but there was no way he would leave his wife in the woods alone and defenseless with the creature out there. "OK, here we go!" He squatted down and said, "Get on my back, Mary!"

"Joe, you can't carry me that far!"

"No debate, just get on!" he responded. Wincing in pain, she got on his back, and he immediately began walking toward the house.

"Almost there, sweetheart. Just another hundred feet or so. We're going to make it!" he said, feeling like a young man again.

"Joe! Joe! I see a red light."

Joe stopped in his tracks. "Where, Mary?"

"It's coming down the driveway; we have to stop!"

"No! We are almost there. Hold on tight; I'm going to try to run."

With Mary on his back, Joe did his best to run at a young man's pace, but he was starting to feel his age coming into play. Stepping into a hole himself, he nearly fell but somehow corrected himself and began running again.

"Joe, the light is getting closer to the house. We are not going to make it!"

"Yes, we will!" Joe was sure he could reach the back door before the creature did.

With seconds to spare, Joe reached the back door and let Mary off his back.

"Joe, we need to get inside now!"

Joe pounded on the door, yelling, "Kids, it's Grandpa; let me in!"

"Joe, it's moving closer!"

"Let us in!" Joe yelled again. Just as he was about to pound on the door again, he heard it unlock, and it swung open. He turned around to grab Mary, but she was gone.

"Mary!" Joe screamed.

"Grandpa! Get inside!" Caleb pleaded.

"Mary, where are you!" he called out.

"Grandpa! Get inside!"

Joe ran off the back porch and into the field, desperately searching the sky and the area for his wife. "Mary!" he called again, but there was no sign of her.

He just stood there. He knew his wife had been taken. "Mary!" he cried.

His grandkids ran outside to get him. "Grandpa! Come inside. We will find her. You can't stay out here. Come on; we must go!" said Beth, pleading with him.

Joe wasn't moving. He was overwhelmed with grief. "Mary! Mary! I've lost her!" he cried. Knowing he wouldn't come in on his own, his grandkids grabbed him by his arms and pulled him into the house.

Fighting them off, Joe ran to the door to go back outside. Caleb beat him there and blocked the doorway. "Grandpa, you can't go out there! I know Grandma was taken, but we need you. Please! Please! Don't go out there!" Caleb pleaded.

Standing eye to eye with Caleb, Joe wanted to remove him so he could get to his wife, but, seeing the desperation and fear in his grandson's eyes, he decided to remain inside the house with his grandkids.

"OK, Caleb, I won't go," said Joe.

"Grandpa, I'm so sorry! Grandma is not the only one who was taken, however!"

"Who else?" asked Joe.

"Melinie was taken, but we got her back. Chase was taken, and we haven't been able to leave, so we can find him. We're also scared that Dad's friend Jay may have been taken too. He was supposed to come by and check on us this weekend, but we haven't heard from him."

Hearing that Chase had been taken hit Joe hard. "Little Chase is gone?" he asked.

"Yes, Grandpa," Caleb responded.

"When? Where?" asked Joe.

"We were on the road home when it happened, Grandpa," Beth said.

"You saw it, sweetheart?"

"Yes," Beth responded tearfully.

Joe put his arms around his granddaughter Beth. Without saying any words, he gave her a long, comforting hug only a loving grandfather could provide. Beth collapsed in his arms and let out a long, deep cry. "I'm here, sweetheart. It'll be OK. It's not your fault," he told Beth.

Melinie was so happy that her grandpa was there with them. He might seem a little gruff sometimes, but they always felt everything would be OK when he was around. Melinie also looked forward to getting a comforting hug from him and approached him.

As she started walking toward him, looking forward to his hug, she suddenly found herself outside the house. "What? Grandpa, where are you?"

"Melinie?" a voice whispered.

"No!" she screamed. She spun around to run to the house but ran straight into an invisible wall. "No, this can't be happening!" Melinie could see into the house. Her family was there but couldn't see or hear her screaming.

Melinie saw herself standing inside with her family. She watched herself walk up to Grandpa and hug him. "No, Grandpa, that's not me!" she screamed. "Grandpa, I'm here; that's not me!"

Still, no one heard her. As she continued to watch, the version of herself inside the house caught her gaze. That Melinie gave her a smirk and sat down on the couch with her brother and sisters.

"This can't be real!" she shouted.

"They can't hear you!" the voice said.

Melinie slowly turned around to see, standing before her, the same creature that had snatched her from her bedroom. "You're not real! This isn't real!" she said, crying.

"Melinie, your time has come! Come with me now!" the creature said.

"Go away!" she hollered.

"Melinie, your soul is joined with mine! You will become as my master foretold it," the creature said.

"What are you talking about? I will not come with you!"

"Come here, Melinie!" the creature demanded.

Like a sheep following the shepherd's voice, Melinie began walking toward the creature. "No! I won't!" she screamed, but her body refused to listen and continued walking in the creature's direction. She was no longer in charge of her body.

When she came within arm's length of the creature, it wrapped her in its wings and flew away with her.

CHAPTER 8

TELL THE STORY

"Grandpa, what is going on?" asked Rachelle.

Joe sat there, lost in his thoughts. He missed his wife so much and could only imagine how scared she might be. It was his fault that she was gone. He didn't protect her and keep her safe. *How can I live without her?* He thought.

I can't believe this is happening again! he thought. Joe was sure this secret would never be brought out and certainly never imagined a world where his grandkids would ever have to deal with the creature as he had.

"Grandpa?" Rachelle tried to get his attention.

"I'm sorry, Rachelle! I'm so sorry!"

"Sorry for what, Grandpa?" asked Beth.

"I'm sorry that this is happening! It's all my fault. I thought the creature was bound forever and would never be free again."

"Bound?" asked Melinie. "What do you mean?"

Joe knew it was time to tell them the story, and he had to put the loss of his wife aside for now so he could be there for his grandkids. He also knew that, unfortunately, they were smack in the middle of this situation and would have no choice but to help him bind the creature again.

"Kids, this happened before over forty years ago. Your grandma and I faced this creature with several others in the community."

"Does it have anything to do with the book?" asked Caleb.

"The book? You found the book?" asked Joe.

Rachelle grabbed the book from the coffee table and handed it to Joe. "We found it downstairs. Beth noticed that your and Grandma's names were written on it. We tried to open it, but it won't," she explained.

Joe looked down at the book and said, "Yes, it's sealed. It cannot be opened without the three other books. When all four are together and the key is in its vicinity, the books will open, and the readers will recite its pages."

"Key? Readers? What are you talking about?" asked Beth.

Binding the creature requires that all the books are together with the key standing in the middle of them. There is so much to tell you all."

"Where are the other books?" asked Melinie.

"They are all hidden in the basement wall next to a symbol like the one on the front cover of this book."

"Yeah, we saw the same symbol downstairs," Caleb said.

"How did you find this book?" asked Joe.

"We didn't. I was alone downstairs, trying to escape the monster, and it just fell onto the floor. When the creature saw it, it took off out the window," said Rachelle.

"That's impossible!" said Joe. "They were all together inside the wall sealed over with concrete. Beth, come with me downstairs; we must see if the other books are still secured inside the wall."

Joe and Beth went to the basement. "Beth, help me move this shelf! There it is! See this patch of concrete? Right here is where we placed the books and sealed them over. I don't know how this one book came to find Rachelle, but she's fortunate that it did!"

"Is it magical, Grandpa?" asked Beth.

"I guess in a way you could say that. Some power or supernatural force is tied to them, but I don't understand their source. I think I was always too afraid to dive any deeper into it. Maybe it's time we searched for a deeper understanding of what we're dealing with here."

"Grandpa, that's blood covering the symbol, right?" asked Beth.

Surprised by her question, Joe said, "Yes, it is. How did you know?"

"Well, the book says, 'Sealed with blood,' so I had to assume that's what it was."

"You assumed correctly."

"Is that your blood?"

Before Joe could answer Beth's question, Rachelle ran down the steps and interrupted the conversation. "No offense, Grandpa, but instead of being down here looking for books, shouldn't we go looking for Grandma and Chase?"

"I wish that were the case, sweetheart; I do! Unfortunately, they don't have a chance without the books."

"But we found Melinie without them," she responded.

"Melinie was taken?" asked Joe.

"Yeah. Don't you remember? We told you that earlier. Caleb and I followed the red light and found her buried under the ground."

Joe didn't recall hearing that Melinie had been taken; hearing about it now, he instantly knew their situation was worse than he had thought. He stood up and looked straight at Melinie. "Melinie, is that you?"

"Grandpa, what do you mean? Of course, it's me."

He told the other kids to get behind him. "Look at me, Melinie!"

She looked away.

"I said, look at me!"

She looked at him, cocked her head to the side, and laughed. "You know they are all mine, Joe," she said.

"Where is my granddaughter?" Joe demanded.

"She's with me, and so is your wife, Mary."

"Let her go!"

"Now, Joe, you know that's not how it works."

"Take me instead!" Joe demanded.

"Only a pureblood can be taken, and your blood has been tainted. Make this easier and bring them all to me. It is the master's will."

"We bound you before, and we will do it again!" Joe reached for the book, but the entity that had taken over Melinie's body blinded him with a bright, red light and disappeared.

"Kids are you OK?" asked Joe.

"Grandpa!" Beth cried. "What just happened? Did the creature possess Melinie again?"

"Again? This happened to Melinie before?" Joe asked.

"Yes, once," said Beth.

"I wish I had known!"

"Where did she go, Grandpa?" Rachelle asked, overcome with emotion.

"With him! She is with him now, kids; I'm sorry!"

"What does that mean?" asked Caleb.

"It means we have a lot to do! All of you, come here." Beth, Rachelle, and Caleb ran to Joe; he wrapped them in his arms, and they all stood there, crying.

After a few minutes, Caleb asked Joe, "Was that Melinie?"

"No, Caleb, it wasn't her. Anyone the creature takes doesn't come back intact. They seem OK at first, but eventually, it takes their soul with the intent to …"

"To what, Grandpa?" asked Beth.

"To make them like him!"

"I can't do this anymore. I just can't!" Beth exclaimed.

"I know this is hard, sweetheart, but you must be strong!"

"Strong? Strong for what? We have no chance of beating this thing! It's too powerful, and we can't do anything to fight this thing! I can't keep doing this; I'm sorry!"

"Beth, you are stronger than you think, and you guys aren't alone anymore. I can beat this thing, but I will need your help."

"How can we help? We know nothing about it. It's at least a step ahead all the time, and apparently, your blood is tainted, so obviously, you can't do anything. So, tell me, how are we going to beat it? Tell me, please!"

Joe walked over to Beth, placed his hands on her shoulders, and smiled at her with that comforting smile that always made her feel better. "Beth, I hear you, and I know that you're scared; so am I, but we can win this fight. I promise!" Those few words and that comforting Grandpa smile made Beth feel a little better. "Sweetheart, do you trust me?"

"Yes, but I have many questions."

"Yes, I know, and now is the time for me to answer some of those.

Come and sit with me; it's time that I share some things you all need to know. All of you, come here and sit with me.

"It was 1978 when this all first happened. Your dad was only five; wow, time went fast!"

"Yeah, he's old now!" Rachelle said with a laugh.

"Yeah, I guess he is," Joe said with a lighthearted laugh. "We had just moved to this house and were so excited to have our own farm. I was concerned with how bad the crime was getting in the city, and when this little place came up for sale, I jumped on it quickly. Your dad and aunts weren't thrilled about it, but the place grew on them after a little while."

"Aunts? We only have one aunt, Grandpa!" Beth said.

"You have another aunt; her name is Brooke."

"So, Valerie isn't your only daughter?" asked Caleb.

"No, I have two daughters, and I will tell you about Brooke a little later."

"Wait, Dad never told us he had another sister!" Beth said.

"I know; that's my fault. I asked him not to."

"Why?" asked Rachelle.

"When I tell you everything I have to say, you will understand why."

"Anyway, one night while watching TV, your grandma and I heard a scream from upstairs. We both ran upstairs to Brooke's room and found her in front of the window. She just stood there screaming. I ran over to her and looked out the window, but all I saw was fog. I asked her what was wrong, but she wouldn't stop screaming.

"Your grandma grabbed her and took her downstairs to see if she could calm her down while I stayed upstairs to see if I could figure out what had scared her so badly. She was looking outside the window when I found her screaming, so I kept looking through it for whatever had caused her fear. The fog was thick, which made it nearly impossible to see anything. After waiting a few minutes and finding nothing, I decided to head back downstairs. As I walked away, I heard this horrible sound that made the hairs on my neck stand straight up.

"I ran back to the window, and this time, I saw something. There it was, looking straight at me, this large creature with wings. It looked like a man but was no man. On its chest was this large, red eye that lit up the fog surrounding it. I immediately jumped back away from the window and ran downstairs. I yelled for your grandma to grab the kids and head to the basement. We stayed downstairs all night, hoping that it wouldn't come inside."

"Did it come inside, Grandpa?" asked Rachelle.

"No, but it terrorized Brooke, Grandma, and me all night long with screams. And it kept calling for us to come outside; it was a real-life nightmare."

"Wait! You didn't mention my dad or Valerie. Did they hear it too?" asked Beth.

"No, and to this day, I still have no idea why not. Maybe it's because they were so young, or … I don't know why they didn't hear it, but I guess I'm thankful they didn't."

"And were they in the basement with you?" asked Rachelle.

"Yes, they were," said Joe.

"And they didn't hear anything?"

"Absolutely nothing, Rachelle!" said Joe.

"How strange!"

"You're telling me!"

"So, our dad was five years old, and Valerie was how old?" asked Beth.

"She would've been around ten at that time."

"That's interesting!" Beth said.

"Yeah, and Brooke would have been about fifteen," Joe added.

"Same age as me," Rachelle said. "But if it's about age, why did it take Chase? He's only five."

"I'm not sure, Rachelle. As I said, I'm not sure why neither your dad nor Valerie heard it."

"Grandpa, have you heard from Mom and Dad since they left for the weekend?" asked Beth.

"I'm sorry, Beth, but no, I haven't. Your grandma called them repeatedly but never got through, so we decided to come here."

"Do you think …"

"I don't want to think that, but more than likely, it has taken them too. Look, kids, as much as I hate this whole situation, I'm going to need your help, and what I'm going to ask you to do will be tough."

"We will do whatever we must to save our parents, Chase, and Melinie," said Caleb.

"I know you will, but first, I must bring you up to speed; let's get started, shall we? Beth, because you're the oldest and have the most experience driving, your part to play will be the most important. I'm going to need you to find your aunt, Brooke."

"How? I'm assuming she's not in the area, I have no car to drive, and it won't let me drive off anyway," she said.

"I understand, sweetheart, but we can't finish what we must do without Brooke. I have my car parked down the road and have a plan. However, let me explain everything to all of you, and then I'll tell you all about my plan."

"OK, Grandpa," said Beth.

"I don't have the time to tell you the whole story, but I must tell you about the creature, the books, and how we bound him the last time. The creature used to be a man, a teenager, to be more exact. We don't have all the details, but we know he was around fifteen in 1899."

"How do you know about him?" asked Caleb.

"I found his journal."

"Journal?"

"Yes, Caleb. Shortly after this all started, I was hunting for the creature in the field when I found this cave. I started to crawl inside to check it out but was stopped by a horrible scream; I assumed it was where the creature lived. As I was backing out, I stumbled over something inside the cave, and there was the journal. I took the book and ran back to the house."

"What did it say? Can we see it?" asked Caleb.

"It started with him talking about his abusive father. Later it talked about the cave I found and how he had become what he is now. Unfortunately, the book went missing, so I couldn't show it to you, but

I remembered enough after reading it to understand what happened to him."

"Where is the cave, Grandpa?" asked Beth.

"I figured you'd ask me that, but that too went missing. I can take you to the exact spot where it was, but it's not there anymore. Is it invisible and can only be seen when he wants us to see it? That's all I can determine."

"Do you think that's where Melinie and the others are?" asked Caleb.

"Yes, I believe so."

"Then we have to go there!" Rachelle demanded.

"That's not our part to play," he said. "The key will go to the cave when it's time."

"We still don't know who or what the key is, Grandpa!" said Beth.

"I will get to that, Beth, but first, let me finish."

"I'm listening!" said Beth.

"According to the journal, this young man—"

"What was his name, Grandpa?" asked Rachelle.

"We couldn't say his name. Did you ever hear him say, 'Say my name'?"

"Yes, yes, we did," Beth said.

"That's because his name was taken from him when he became the creature, and part of what drives him is the desire to know it. We don't fully understand why, but if you say his name, something else is also unleashed, and we cannot allow that to happen. To protect you, I will not tell you his name; I'm sorry!"

"I don't understand, but we'll trust you, Grandpa."

"Thank you, Beth."

"When the creature was a young man, he suffered much abuse from his father. He explained that it was so bad that on one occasion, his father even broke his legs for disrespecting him."

"That's awful!" said Caleb.

"I agree! Long story short, he heard a voice calling from the woods one night. When he went out to find out where it was coming from, he was led to the cave by way of a red, glowing light. Eventually, he went inside, and that's where he met what he referred to as 'his master.' This thing or entity explained that he could save him from his father and promised to give him great power. What he didn't tell him was that he would become something else. He was forced to drink the master's blood and through extreme torture entered a dark covenant with it, which turned him into the creature. His will was taken from him, and he became the 'unnamed and unwritten,' never to be the man he was before."

"What is the thing that turned him?" asked Caleb.

"That is very hard to explain. It is one of the 'Old Ones,' a dark entity somehow bound to the cave."

"By what and for what reason?"

"We don't know."

"Is it still in the cave?" asked Beth.

"We don't think so. In his journal, he writes that the master left him. We can only assume that the ritual not only changed the young man but also freed the dark being."

"How is any of this real?" asked Rachelle.

"I don't know, but it's real, and we have to stop it again," said Joe. He grabbed the book. "Now, I need to explain the books."

CHAPTER 9

THE BOOKS

Joe turned the book over and showed them the back cover. "I know it's a little hard to make out, but there are eight names written here: mine, your grandmother's, and the names of six other couples sharing the same last name. Each last name mentioned here also represents four homes where the books and symbols like the one you saw downstairs are located. Each home acts as a type of conduit, and when all four symbols are in place, the key will release the 'readers,' who ultimately allow the binding of the creature. Do you follow so far?"

"I think so, Grandpa," Beth said; the other two nodded in agreement.

"OK, good."

"I have a question?" asked Caleb. "What does the symbol represent?"

"I was just getting to that," said Joe.

"OK, sorry. Go on."

"The symbol represents what happens when the key is activated. Once that happens, it is transformed into a hunter that fights the creature, ultimately stripping it of its power and throwing it into an impenetrable cage. Once the creature is caged, the cave opens, and the creature is bound inside with no way to escape. The cave disappears, only to be made visible again if the creature is released."

"If it can't escape, how did it get out?" asked Beth.

"Well, it can only happen if one of the symbols has been damaged."

"Is that what happened?" asked Caleb.

"Yes, it did; on our way here, we saw that one of the homes that carried a symbol had been torn down, and the symbol was gone."

"What about the other symbols? Are they gone too?" asked Beth.

"I'm not sure, but they may have been damaged; I'm not sure," said Joe.

"If they're still there, how do we know if they've been damaged?" asked Rachelle.

"The blood covering the symbol would have had to be removed or affected somehow. Without checking on them, there's no way to know."

"Can't we just find out who bought the property and ask if they have the symbol that was taken?" asked Caleb.

"I wish it was that easy. Even if we found it, there's a good chance that the blood had been removed."

"Are the other homes still standing?" asked Caleb.

"I didn't have time to check on them; your grandma and I had to get here as soon as possible."

"Oh, great! We don't have all the symbols and the blood that activated them. So, what now?" Beth asked.

"We must create a new symbol for that house, and we need to check on the other two as well."

"Oh, no problem. Let's go now and see how quickly it catches us!" Beth replied with frustration and sarcasm.

"Beth! You're not helping!" Rachelle responded.

"I'm sorry, but this sounds like a no-win situation; how else am I supposed to act?"

"Beth, I know this is hard. It's not what any of us wants to do or planned for, but if we work together, we can get this done; trust me," said Joe.

"Grandpa, if it cannot enter the homes that have the symbols, then I don't understand something. It was when I was at Zack's house."

"Who's Zack?"

"He found me on the road and helped me; the creature took him, though!"

"I'm sorry, Beth!"

Beth started to cry and took a moment to compose herself. "Thank you, Grandpa! The creature appeared at his house but acted like it couldn't go in. It kept looking at the top of the door. Are there other symbols or something?"

"Yes. Only four symbols activate the books, but some people in the community carved that same symbol above the doors of their homes. I wasn't sure if it worked, but it does sound like it might have from what you're telling me."

"Grandpa, I have a question too," said Rachelle.

"Go ahead, Rachelle!"

"So, when I was in the basement, the fog came in through the windows, and the creature entered the house; it nearly got me. If the symbol protects this house, how did it get inside?"

Joe scratched his head and said, "That makes no sense! Did you see it?"

"Yes!"

"Well, what happened?"

"Like I said earlier, when I was trying to kick at it, one book fell on the basement floor. When the creature saw it, it screamed and flew out the window."

"Rachelle, I don't have a definite answer, but I can only think that if the fog can get inside, it may allow the creature to make it inside too. But that is only my hypothesis."

"Well, I guess we need to ensure there's no way for the fog to get inside, Grandpa."

"I think you're right! We need to seal up that window."

"We need to seal up more than just that one, Grandpa," said Rachelle. "The creature broke all the windows out before it flew out the window."

"OK, we will get them all sealed up," said Joe.

"So, what's the plan?" asked Caleb.

"We all have a part to play. Beth will find Brooke and bring her back here. Caleb, I need you to check on the other two homes, and Rachelle, well, you will have to provide the blood."

"What? What do you mean? Are you planning to sacrifice me or something? I am not down for giving my life."

"No, sweetheart, that's not what I mean. If the other symbols are intact, we must use just a tiny amount of blood to reactivate the symbol we have to remake. I promise it won't be a big deal, but it must be done."

"What about your blood, Grandpa?"

"I would do it in a heartbeat, but the creature was right when it said through Melinie's body that my blood had been tainted. My blood was used before, and only one whose blood is pure can be used. Once one's blood has been mingled with the symbol, it cannot be used again."

"Oh, lucky me!" Rachelle said while rolling her eyes.

"I'm sorry, Rachelle, I am."

"That's fine. Let's do this."

"OK," said Joe. "Beth, you're up first. Let's go over the plan to find Brooke."

"Grandpa, why do we need to find Brooke?" asked Beth.

"She's the key," said Joe.

"She's the key that fights the creature?"

"That's right, Beth! Without her, we can't bind him!"

"Does she know this?"

"She does, and that's the hardest part. You asked if she knew about any of you. Unfortunately, when she transformed, she lost all connections with the family except with me. The key and the 'blood giver' form a bond that cannot be broken and always have a connection, but while I kept my connections with Brooke, everyone else became a stranger to her."

"Did you try to help her remember?"

"I did, but she saw something else when she looked at any of them."

"What did she see?"

"Blank faces."

"You mean like they were just unfamiliar to her?"

"No, I mean blank faces with no distinguishable features."

"That must have been awful for her!"

"It was. They looked like monsters to her. Just a glance at them

caused her to panic and cry. I was the only person who looked normal
to her."

"What happened to her?"

Joe looked down and struggled to speak.

"Grandpa?"

"Brooke couldn't handle it. She couldn't function, and we had to
place her in a mental hospital."

"Is she still there?"

"She was up until last year. I visited her every week since it happened,
and there seemed to be no positive changes. Then, out of nowhere, I
received a call from the hospital. The doctor said that she had woken up
and acted like a different person that morning. I immediately drove up
to see her, and he was right. She seemed to be in her right mind. After a
few months of therapy and observation, she was released."

"Where is she now?"

"That's the good news! A friend of mine owns a little antique shop
in town with a loft upstairs. He gave her a job, and she rents the loft
from him."

"That's great!"

"Yeah but convincing her to return here will not be easy."

"Does she remember what happened?"

"She does. But if it were you, would you want to go through that
again, Beth?"

"No, I definitely would not! So, what's the plan?"

"You can't tell her who you are. That's for sure!"

"OK, I get that. So, how do I get her here?"

"Beth, I hate to ask this of you, but you'll have to lie to her."

"Well, desperate times require desperate measures, right?"

"True!"

"What do I tell her?"

"I'm not entirely sure. I was hoping that maybe you could come up
with something. Maybe tell her I'm sick or about to die and that she
needs to come now."

"Grandpa, I can't tell her that!"

"It has to be something urgent, or she won't come. Please, Beth!"

"OK, OK, I'll come up with something, but how do I get there?"

Joe told Beth to follow the same path to the car he and his wife, Mary had used to get to the house. He provided the address and directions to the antique store and handed her the car keys. "Be careful and hide in the grass if you see the red light. If you see the fog heading toward you, run as fast as possible until you reach the car."

"I wish you were going with me, Grandpa!"

"I do too, sweetheart. I do too. Now, I'm going to create a distraction while you head out the back door. I will open the front door and start yelling for the creature. When you hear me yell, it's time to go."

"Understood, Grandpa!"

"Good luck, my little Beth!"

"Thank you!"

Beth reached the back door and waited for Joe's distraction. "Come and get me!" Joe yelled. That was Beth's cue.

Immediately, Beth ran outside and followed Joe's directions to the car. "Crap, I forgot to grab a flashlight!" she exclaimed. She grabbed her phone and turned on the flashlight app. "Much better!" she whispered. Beth followed the creek down to the tree line as Joe had instructed.

As she approached the tree line, she looked toward the house for any sign of the fog or the red light. Fog surrounded the house, and she could see the red light darting up and down over the place. *Good, it doesn't see me!* she thought. *There's the car!* Beth clicked unlock on the key fob and stepped inside the car. Before starting the car, she took another look to ensure the creature was still hovering over the house and not headed her way; it was still there.

Fortunately, Joe had parked the car far enough away that she could start it and hopefully drive away without it noticing her. Beth started the car and made sure to keep the headlights turned off. She then slowly pulled the car around and headed to town, waiting to turn the lights on until she was out of view.

What am I going to tell Brooke? Beth wondered. She ran several scenarios in her head, all of which sounded ridiculous to her. "Isn't this how life works? I get to meet my long-lost aunt for the first time, only to lie to her. I love Grandpa, but how can I do this to her? She went through so many years of mental torment, and I'm the one who will bring her back home to make her go through it all over again; this just isn't right!"

As Beth passed the Salt Hills city limits sign, she felt sick. "How can I go through with this?" she asked herself. "I'm just going to turn around and tell Grandpa there has to be a different way." As she slowed the car down to turn left back toward the house, another vehicle hit her in the rear end. The impact caused her to hit her head, knocking her out cold.

Hours later, Beth woke up with a nurse looking down at her. "Well, hello, sweetheart! Glad to see you're finally awake!"

"Where am I?"

"You're in the hospital, sweetie. You were rear-ended, and the ambulance brought you here a few hours ago."

"The hospital?" Beth asked.

"Yes, dear! But don't worry; you'll be OK. We're keeping you under observation to ensure you don't have a concussion."

"Who hit me?"

"Well, she's right outside. She felt so bad about it and wanted to ensure you were OK. Is it OK if she comes in to talk to you?"

"Uh, yeah, I guess so," said Beth.

"OK, I'll go get her. I need to check on another patient, but if you need anything, just hit the call button, OK?"

"OK, thank you!"

After the nurse left the room, the lady walked in. Beth didn't know her, but somehow, she seemed familiar. "Hi, how are you feeling?" the lady asked.

"I think I'm doing OK."

"Good! Look, I'm so sorry for running into you. It was getting foggy, and I didn't see you until it was too late; I'm very sorry!"

"Did you say it was foggy?"

"Yes, the fog just came out of nowhere, making it hard to see."

"I didn't see any fog!" Beth responded.

"That's odd! Maybe it was clear in front of your car, which doesn't make much sense, but anyway, I just wanted to check on you and say I'm very sorry! I'll let you get some rest."

As the lady turned to walk away, Beth asked, "Wait. How far am I from Salt Hills?"

"About thirty minutes."

"Do you know if my car is drivable and where it is? I need to get back there as soon as possible."

"I don't think it is. The tow truck was loading it up while the EMS was preparing to take you here; I'm sorry!"

"I really must get back; it's an emergency! I know you don't know me, but is there any way you could give me a ride?"

"But you might have a concussion or something. Don't you think you need to let them finish examining you before you leave?"

"I can't, and I feel fine. Besides, you'll be driving, not me. Please, I must get back to Salt Hills."

The lady paused momentarily, then said, "OK, it's the least I can do, but promise me, if you start feeling sick, you'll let me drive you back here."

"I promise!"

"OK, we'll have to move fast before the nurse returns. Here are your clothes. I'll watch the door as you put them on."

"Thank you! By the way, what's your name? Mine is Beth."

"I'm Brooke; nice to meet you. Now hurry!"

Brooke? Is this my aunt? Is this really her? Beth wondered.

"Beth, what are you doing? You need to hurry!"

Beth stood there in a state of shock. "I'm sorry! I was just—"

"That's OK; we must get out of here before the nurse returns."

"You're right!" Beth hurried to put her clothes on, trying to process this potential stroke of luck. "OK, I'm ready!"

Brooke looked both ways down the hall. "It's clear. Let's go!" Beth and Brooke made their way down the hall to exit the hospital.

"There's my car. It got slightly banged up but seemed to be running fine." They both climbed inside and headed out of the hospital parking lot. "Where am I taking you?" asked Brooke. what

"Just head into town, and I'll show you where to go."

"Sounds good. I hope I don't get in trouble for this!" Brooke said.

"Don't worry; I won't turn you in!" said Beth with a chuckle.

"I appreciate that! I've had enough trouble in my life!" Brooke said with a shrug.

As Brooke and Beth arrived in town, Brooke asked Beth where she needed to drop her off. With butterflies filling her stomach, Beth said, "At the antique shop."

Brooke pulled off to the side of the road and stopped the car. "The antique shop! What is this? What kind of game are you playing? That's where I live."

"I know, Brooke; let me explain."

Brooke turned off the car, put her arm over the passenger side headrest, and with a harsh stare said, "You have thirty seconds!"

Beth let out a deep sigh. "I am your niece."

"What? I don't have a niece!"

"Give a second to explain, please! It's a very long story, and I don't have time to tell you everything. But your dad, my grandpa, sent me here to find you."

"Is he OK?"

"For now, yes, but there is an emergency at the farm, and he needs you to come there right now!"

Brooke positioned herself back in the driver's seat and said softly, "I knew this day would come."

"You did?"

"Yes! It's back, isn't it?"

Beth didn't know what to say. *Does she remember what happened? How does she know it's back?* she wondered. "Are you talking about …?"

"Yes, Beth, I'm talking about the creature. It's back, isn't it?"

"Yes. It's back!"

"Has it taken anyone?"

Trying her best not to cry, Beth responded, "Yes, it has taken at least three I know of and probably more."

Brooke just sat there silently.

"Brooke?"

"I'll go with you," said Brooke.

"You will?"

"Yes!"

"Are you sure? I know what you went through. I had decided not to ask you, and right before you hit me, I was turning the car around."

"That has to be a sign."

"A sign?" Beth asked.

"How else can you explain it? What is the likelihood that you came to find me and that it was me who hit you? Why did I decide to go to the hospital? How is it that you asked me for a ride before knowing who I was? You didn't know, right?"

"No, I didn't. I wasn't even positive after you told me your name. I mean, how can that happen?"

"Exactly! I must go, Beth, and we both know it."

"I guess so!" said Beth.

"Well, what are we waiting for?"

"Are you sure, Brooke? We can try to find another way."

"There's no other way but thank you. All I ask is that you will fill me in on something."

"OK, what's that?"

"Tell me about you and the family while we drive to the farm."

"I can do that. I'll give you a quick rundown on the way to the farm, and once this is over, I'll tell you the rest. Deal?"

"Deal!"

"I can't believe I have a brother, a sister, three nieces, and two nephews! I can't wait to meet them all!"

"Do you remember your mother, Brooke?"

"No!"

"She was taken too! Do you remember seeing people without faces when you were little?"

"Yes! It was horrible. They looked like monsters."

"They weren't monsters, Brooke; they were your family. After the creature was bound, your memories and connections with all your family except Grandpa were taken from you."

"They were my family?"

"Yes, and I'm afraid that when this is all over, the same thing may happen again, and that's why I was scared to ask you to come."

"There's the farm, Beth!"

"Brooke, we need to talk more about what might happen if you do this."

"Later! Let's get to the farm and worry about that later."

"Brooke?"

"It's OK, Beth. Let's talk later, OK?"

"OK! Stop over there, Brooke. That's where we get out and walk the rest of the way."

Brooke pulled the car off to the side of the road and turned off the lights. "You lead the way, Beth; it's been too long ago for me to remember."

"OK. Before we go, let's see if the fog and the creature are still surrounding the house. I told Grandpa we'd use some sign to let him know we were here so he could create another diversion."

"What sign?"

"He said to just come up with one, so I don't know."

"No worries. I have just the one."

Brooke cupped her hands around her mouth and made this loud birdlike sound. "What was that?" Beth asked.

"It's the sound of a bird I used to hear when I was little. I used to drive my dad crazy with it. I'd do it daily to get on his nerves; he'll remember it."

"Over here, you ugly beast!" Joe shouted.

"Guess you were right."

While Joe kept the creature busy by screaming at it, Beth and Brooke made their way to the house. "It's working! Let's move faster!" Beth told Brooke. "Brooke?"

Brooke wasn't moving. "Wait, stop!" said Brooke.

"What is it?" Beth asked.

"Something is out here with us."

Beth stopped to listen and heard rustling in the leaves. "What is it?" Beth asked.

"Quiet!" said Brooke.

"Beth, help me!" a familiar voice called.

"Melinie?" Beth asked.

"Beth, I escaped," Melinie said, "and I need your help."

"Where are you?"

"I'm over here. Please help me!"

Beth stepped off the path to help her sister Melinie, but Brooke grabbed her arm. "Beth, what are you doing?"

"It's my sister Melinie. She's calling out to me!"

"Beth, that's not your sister. It's the creature trying to lure you in. It knows we're here. We must go now!"

"But what if it's really her?"

"Is she calling to you now?"

"Yes, can't you hear her?"

"No, I can't, and why do you think that is? It's a trap. Come on; we must go before it is too late."

Beth knew Brooke was probably right, but how could she leave her sister without knowing for sure? "Melinie, if that's you, come out and let me see you," Beth said.

"I can't; it will see me!"

"I'll keep you safe; just let me see your face."

"Beth, help me, please!"

"Beth, stop!" Brooke said. "If it was your sister, wouldn't she come out?"

"I-I-I guess so."

Brooke grabbed Beth's arm again and pulled her. "Come on, let's go!"

Beth listened to Brooke and got back on the path. "I'm sorry, sis, I can't come to you!"

"We will come to you, Beth! My master will find you!" Melinie shouted.

"Oh, my God!" Beth yelled.

"Run!" Brooke shouted.

Beth and Brooke took off toward the house, running as fast as they could. As they approached the house, the fog made its way toward them. "We're not going to make it!" Beth yelled.

"Just keep running!" yelled Brooke.

Swoosh!

The creature flew over their heads, barely missing them as they ducked into the tall grass. "Lie on your belly!" said Brooke. "We will hide inside the grass. We will have to crawl the rest of the way."

"What about its red eye, Brooke? If it shines on the grass, it will find us."

"You're right, Beth. We need help!" Brooke made the same call with her mouth as before.

"Immediately, they heard Joe yelling at the creature again. However, this time, he took it a step further.

Boom!

"What was that?" asked Beth. "It sounds like a rifle."

Joe ran into the field before the house and began firing off rounds at the creature. "Run, girls!" he shouted.

"There's our cue!" said Brooke. "Run, Beth!"

The two girls ran hand in hand toward the house. Every time the creature got close to them, Joe fired a round, hitting the beast. None of the shots injured the monster, but they knocked it off course, enough to keep the girls safe.

"Head to the back door!" Joe shouted. He fired the gun again.

Boom!

After nearly getting snatched up by the creature, Beth and Brooke reached the back door and stepped inside.

"Grandpa!" Beth shouted as she ran up and hugged Joe.

"You girls, OK?"

"Yes, I think so!" said Beth.

"Brooke! My sweet girl!" he said. "It's so good to see you!"

"Hi, Dad!"

"Come give me a hug, sweetheart!"

Brooke hugged Joe and said, "Dad, I have so many questions about—"

"I know you do, and I promise I will tell you everything, but we must focus on dealing with the creature right now." He turned to Beth. "Beth, thank you for bringing her here!"

"You're welcome, and do I have a story to tell you about how!"

"Hold it for now, but I can't wait to hear it!"

"Grandpa, where is Caleb?" Beth asked.

"It was taking a long time for you to get back, so I decided to go ahead and send him out; he left a couple of hours ago."

"Is he OK?"

"I hope so! He got out without being seen. I created another diversion, and so far, so good."

"When will he be back?"

"Well, without another car to use, he had to take Rachelle's bike, so It'll be a while."

Caleb followed the map Joe had made to the first house on the list. "Yes!" He saw that the house was still standing, and the lights were on. "Well, one down and just one more to go!" he said to himself.

Man, it's dark out here! he thought. He took out his flashlight to view the map to head to the next house on the list. "OK, it looks like it's about five miles away. Geez, I wish I had a car!"

As Caleb started to pedal away, he heard what sounded like someone tapping on a window. Looking over at the house, he saw a little boy standing at the window. "Oh, it's just a little boy. What's he doing?"

The boy looked afraid and pointed toward something behind Caleb. Caleb turned to look behind him, and there, standing behind him, was his sister Melinie.

From the shock, Caleb nearly fell off his bike. "Mel?"

"Hi, brother!" she said with an awkward smile.

"Is that really you?"

"Yes! I need your help! Come here!" she said.

"Mel, I'm afraid!"

"Don't be afraid! Come here, please!"

Caleb was too afraid to go to his sister. He remembered what had happened at the house and thought the creature might have possessed her again.

"I must leave, sis; I can't help you right now!"

"Come here, Caleb!"

"No!" Caleb jumped on the bike and pedaled as fast as he could away from her. While pedaling away, he looked back and saw she was gone. "This is bad. This is so bad!" he said.

Swoosh!

"What was that?"

"Caleb!" Melinie called out.

"Leave me alone!"

"Caleb!" she called again.

Suddenly, the bike stopped. Melinie appeared in front of him with her hands on the handlebars. "I can't let you leave, brother. The master has asked for you."

"Melinie, it's me. Don't do this!"

Melinie looked into Caleb's eyes. She tilted her head a little, then with a smile said, "It is time!" She let out a scream that paralyzed Caleb.

Unable to move but completely aware, he watched as his sister began to transform. Talons began growing from her fingertips, and wings formed from her back. Her eyes changed from their current color to a dark black. She now towered high above him. She looked at him again but now with those black eyes.

He tried to scream, but nothing happened. Without a sound, she dug her talons into his shoulders; the pain was excruciating. She then wrapped her newly found wings around his body like a cocoon and lifted him high into the sky. As he was taken away, the child at the window stood screaming, but no one saw or heard what had happened.

"It's been too long; something's happened!" said Joe.

"Why did you send him alone, Grandpa?" asked Rachelle.

"I'm sorry, but it was the only way!"

"What now?" asked Beth.

"We must assume that the other two symbols have also been damaged, so we must remake them. Brooke, I need you to—"

"I know, Dad. I need to get ready!"

"I'm so sorry, sweetheart. I never thought we'd have to do this again."

"It's OK, Dad. You can apologize later; we need to get this done."

"OK!"

"Rachelle, I hate to tell you this, but we need more blood than we first intended. Without knowing if the other two homes are still standing, we need enough to cover three symbols instead of just one."

"Oh great! OK, then," said Rachelle. "So you know, I've never even given blood before because I'm afraid of needles. So, if I pass out, it's not my fault."

Beth looked at her sister and said, "I'll be with you, sis; it'll be OK. I promise."

"I'm holding you to that."

"Does anyone know how to make pottery?" asked Joe.

"I took a pottery class once, but you don't want to see how it turned out," Beth said with a chuckle.

"Well, you won't be making a pot, so the job is yours," said Joe with a smile.

"Lucky me! Grandpa, I have a question," said Beth. "Did you write these books, and how did you figure all of this out?"

"No, I didn't write them. Back when this problem started with our family, there was an elderly gentleman who showed up at the house with books in his hand. He didn't introduce himself or say how he knew the creature was tormenting us. He said only that the books would guide us on how to stop it. With that, he handed me the books and some handwritten instructions and left; we never saw him again, Beth."

"Who do you think he was?"

"I can't say. After the strange visit was over, I asked around the community to see if anyone might know the man, but no one had any clue."

"That's really strange!"

"I agree. Even stranger is the fact that he didn't drive up in a car, and when I turned to ask him a question, he just disappeared."

"Disappeared?"

"Yeah, crazy, huh?"

"Definitely! That gives me goosebumps!" Beth said.

"Me too!"

"Ready to put your pottery skills into action?"

"Guess so!"

"OK, let's get started."

Joe took a large piece of paper and began drawing the template for the symbol Beth needed to make with the exact size and scope required. In the middle of the drawing was a key, but it didn't look like a key; it looked like a four-winged creature with the sun surrounding it. Two wings pointed up, and two wings pointed down. Each wing pointed toward an object in each corner of the drawing. The objects resembled homes or a structure of some sort. Lastly, at the bottom of the picture, what looked like a cage or cell was being held by talons on the creature's feet.

Beth looked at Brooke with saddened eyes, then turned to Joe and asked, "Is that creature what Brooke will look like when she transforms?"

"Yes, it is."

"I feel so bad for her."

"Me too, Beth. I wish there were another way."

Changing the subject, Beth asked, "Grandpa, have you ever seen any of my art projects? I am not an artist. I can't make this look like you're drawing."

"It's OK, Beth. Our symbols were not perfect either. According to the books, the symbols need to be on there, but the most important thing is that they are the exact dimensions I drew out for you and that the wings point toward the objects. If we have those measurements right, we are golden."

"I certainly hope so," said Beth.

"Rachelle, come with me!" Rachelle followed Joe to the basement. "We need to get the books out of the wall, and I need your help."

"OK, Grandpa, how can I help?"

Joe handed Rachelle a hammer. "I need you to use the claw side of this hammer to chip away at this section of the basement wall; that's where they're at."

"Got it, Grandpa!"

"While you're doing that, I will get some boards and cover up the broken windows."

After an hour or so of chipping, the wall crumbled away. "Grandpa, I think I'm done!"

Joe reached inside the hole, now exposed, and pulled out a metal box. After opening it, he pulled out three books, which looked identical to the one Rachelle had found earlier. "Want to know something else that's strange, Rachelle?"

"What's that?"

"I told this to Beth earlier and still can't explain it. The book you found had also been in this box."

"How is that possible?"

"That's the million-dollar question. Now watch this." Joe laid the four books on the floor, and immediately they linked together, then opened simultaneously.

"Wow! How in the world?" Rachelle said.

"Freaky, huh?"

"That's not the word I was going to use!" she said, laughing. "Now what?"

"Your sister starts on the symbols."

CHAPTER 10

THE SYMBOLS

After a few hours of her best work, Beth was done with the symbols. *Not bad!* she thought as she admired her work. "But I don't have a kiln for a bisque firing. I can't believe I remembered that term. I guess I did learn something after all," she said to herself, laughing. Laying them on the table to bone dry, she left to find Joe.

"Grandpa, the symbols are ready, but we don't have a kiln!"

"I made one, and it should still be out there in the barn."

Beth stared at Joe. "You made one, and it's in the barn?"

"Oh yeah, that's a problem, huh?"

"Do you think they'll work if they are not fired?"

"Guess we'll have to find out, Beth! But that's not the only issue."

"What now!"

"So, remember the symbol and how four structures are positioned in four different spots?"

"Yeah?"

"Well, each house selected was in the exact spot the books identified as areas where the symbols needed to be placed."

"I see!"

"Yeah!"

"So, what you're telling me is that we will have to take each of them to those exact places for this to work, right?"

With an uncomfortable-sounding laugh, Joe said, "Yes, we will."

"Of course we do! Any other surprises I need to know about?"

Joe shrugged and said, "I'm sure something else will come up!"

"Undoubtedly!"

"So, who is the lucky person who gets the job of taking the symbols to the three homes?" asked Beth.

"We are one for two so far, not the best of odds!" said Beth.

"And without them being fired, what if they fall apart while trying to get them there?"

"I will make the trip since I know where they are," said Joe.

"If you go, who's going to read the books?"

"No one will, Beth."

"What do you mean?"

"Look!" Joe showed Beth the first page. "See, this page shows the symbols, how they're made, and summarizes using the blood. But look at this!" He turned to the next page.

"What language is that?"

"I have no idea! But when the blood-covered symbols are in place and the key is readied, the pages turn on their own, and you can hear disembodied voices reading it."

"Is that what you meant when you mentioned the readers?"

"Yes, it is!"

"Grandpa, that is scary!"

"I know it is! Once all the pages are turned, the key, Brooke, becomes what you see on the drawing, and the creature becomes bound again to the cave."

"This is too much to take in, Grandpa!"

"I know, sweetheart!"

"I never believed in the supernatural before, and now I'm living it. I am second-guessing everything I have ever believed."

"Me too! I don't understand any of this," he said. "Who are the disembodied voices? Is it God or some supernatural higher power?"

"I can only assume! I never really believed in a higher power, but I can't deny that whatever this is, it must be beyond our understanding. What that means isn't clear to me. You're sure this is going to work?"

"Yes!"

"OK, well, what's your plan to get the symbols to the other locations?"

"Do you know how to shoot a rifle Beth?"

"Yeah, my dad taught me, but it's been a while!"

"Good! I hope you're a good shot because my escape plan depends on you making each shot count."

"Of course, it does!" Beth said, rolling her eyes. "Where's the gun, Grandpa?"

As Beth practiced holding the rifle to get comfortable, she noticed Rachelle walking back and forth, talking to herself. "Rachelle, are you OK?" Beth asked.

"Oh yeah, just great! I can't wait to get sliced open so my blood can be drained out; I'm so excited about it!"

"Sis, I know you're scared, but Grandpa wouldn't do anything to hurt you."

"I know, but I'm still scared, and what if it doesn't work? What if nothing works, and we never see Mom or Dad again, or we end up being taken too?"

"Rachelle, I'm scared too, and if I can be honest, I don't know what will happen. But if there's one person I trust, it's Grandpa. We must believe he knows what he's doing and do what he says to do."

"I know. I've just never been so scared in my life!"

"Me either, sis, me either."

"Brooke are you ready for this?" asked Joe.

"Do I have a choice, Dad?"

"You know this isn't what I want, right?"

"I know, Dad, but what choice do we have?"

Joe looked away to hide his tears.

"Dad, is Beth right about the monsters I saw as a kid being my family?"

"Yes, she is right!"

"So much was taken from me, Dad! I spent years thinking I was an only child, and now I find out nearly forty years later that I have two siblings and that my mom was here the whole time. It just isn't fair!"

Joe put his arms around Brooke and let her cry into his shoulder. "I'm so sorry, my sweet girl! No, none of this is fair. If you're not up to doing this, we will find another way."

"No, Dad, we know there's not. We must do this. Just do me a favor. If I lose my memory again and my family looks like monsters to me, please just let me go and keep my family away from me. I can't go through that again!"

"I will do what's right, sweetheart, but not all of your family may look that way."

"What do you mean?"

"Well, you remembered me, right?"

"Yeah."

"That's because the one whose blood activates the symbols somehow becomes linked to you. So, if it happens again, you may not recognize me this time." Joe began tearing up. "But it would be Rachelle; you will remember her."

"I can't lose you, Dad!"

"You won't, but I will ensure she's the one you see first. After it's all over, she will ask you what you remember; if you remember me, we know it will be OK. If you do not, we will stay away until we find a way to remove the curse or whatever it is that removes your memory and causes the changes in your family's faces; I promise we will find a way."

"I hope so, Dad, I hope so!"

"Grandpa, how will we know if the symbols are in place and that it's time for Brooke to become the key?" asked Rachelle.

"So, the books are linked together in the form of a star, which leaves a place for Brooke to stand in the middle of them. Once the symbols are in place, the blood activates them. Then, as soon as Brooke stands in the middle of them, you will hear four distinct voices reading from each of them in unison, and then you will see Brooke transform into what you see here on the drawing."

"Grandpa, how did you discover Brooke was the key?" asked Beth.

"It was on the handwritten page that the man gave me. It said that, that person would enter a trance-like state when the chosen one touched the book. During this trance, a mark in the shape of a key will appear on that person's side."

"Does she have the mark, and does it look like a key?"

Overhearing the conversation, Brooke said, "Yes, Beth! Here, look for yourself!" Brooke lifted her shirt just enough so Beth could see the mark."

"Wow, it looks like a burn. Did it hurt?"

"It did and still does sometimes!"

"I'm sorry, Brooke!"

"It is what it is! Dad, that's what I become?" asked Brooke.

"Yes, you don't remember?"

"No, not at all! I remember being surrounded by light, hearing voices, then waking up outside."

"Maybe that's a good thing!"

"What is it like when you transform?" asked Rachelle.

"As I said, I don't remember it happening. All I can recall are the nightmares afterward."

"I'm so sorry!" Rachelle responded.

"It's OK! I'm just hoping this time that I'll remember all of you," Brooke said. "I missed so much; I want to know my family!"

"I hope so too!"

"OK, Beth," Joe said, "how comfortable are you with the rifle? Ready to go hunting?"

"As ready as I'll ever be!"

"Good enough, I guess."

"Grandpa, I wrapped the symbols up tight with plastic wrap. I hope they stay together for you!"

"I'm sure they will! Now, we need the blood."

Everyone turned and looked at Rachelle.

"Oh, I guess it's my turn. Oh, man! OK, do it fast!"

"I will be as gentle as possible, but I can't promise it won't hurt Rachelle!" said Joe.

"Just do it already before I change my mind!"

"OK, sweetheart!"

Joe grabbed his knife and a mason jar from the kitchen cabinet. "Here, bite down on this." Joe gave her a towel, which had been folded and twisted up.

"Beth, can you get me a warm water bowl and another towel?"

"Yes, Grandpa."

"And Brooke, please get the first aid kit under the bathroom sink."

"Got it, Dad!"

After cleaning his knife with alcohol, he asked Beth and Brooke to keep Rachelle still. "Turn your head, kiddo, so you don't see. I know this doesn't help, but the knife is very sharp, and that will help keep the pain down."

"OK, Grandpa."

Rachelle winced and whimpered in pain as Joe sliced the inside of her palm about two inches. He then turned her hand with the palm facing down over the mason jar to allow it to fill up. "Almost done, kiddo; you're doing great! OK, that should be good. Keep your head turned, Rachelle, as we bandage your hand up."

Joe then cleaned her wound with warm water and bandaged her hand. "All done, Rachelle; you can look now."

"Glad that's over!" said Rachelle.

"You did great. I'm proud of you," said Joe.

"Thank you, Grandpa!"

"Is there a backpack I can use?" asked Joe.

"Yeah, I have my school backpack," Rachelle responded. "I'll go get it."

After getting the backpack from Rachelle, Joe carefully filled it with the symbols; and after taping up the mason jar with duct tape, he also placed it inside. "Well, I've got all I need; I guess it's up to me and your sharpshooting skills, Beth," said Grandpa with a chuckle. "I hope you can still run fast."

Beth responded with a nervous laugh. "Me too."

"Dad, be careful," said Brooke.

"I will," he said as he hugged her.

"Grandpa, do you think it'll work again? We tricked him twice, but what if he's onto us this time?" asked Rachelle.

"I just have to believe it will; besides, there are no other options."

"Dad, what if we camouflage you?" Brooke said.

"I'm listening!"

"Does my brother hunt? Like, does he have any camo?"

"Yeah, he does!" said Rachelle. "I've seen him wear it. They're probably hanging up in the closet."

"Nice thinking, Brooke!" said Joe.

They all went upstairs to Mark and Amber's room. "There they are!" said Rachelle. Mark had camo pants, a shirt, and even a jacket.

"This is great!" Joe grabbed the clothes, went into the bathroom, and changed into them. After leaving the bathroom, he said, "Well, how do I look?"

"Good, but you're missing something!" said Rachelle. She went into the bathroom and came out with a couple of bottles of mascara. "We need to hide your face!"

"Now you're thinking!"

The girls emptied the mascara bottles onto their hands and covered Joe's face. "Now, we're talking!" said Beth.

"OK, I think we're all set!" said Joe. He walked to the back door. "Beth, are you ready?"

"I'm ready!" She positioned the rifle on her shoulder and aimed at the front door.

"Here we go!" Joe opened the door just slightly to get a position on the creature. "Looks like he's flying over the front fields, so now is the time."

"Wait, Grandpa," said Beth. "How will you see through the fog? It's everywhere!"

"I know this place like the back of my hand. I could make my way blindfolded; I'll be OK! Now, let's do this!"

Taking a quick look outside to ensure it was clear to go, Joe bolted off the back porch and headed toward the creek.

After opening the front door, Beth stepped inside the doorway with the rifle pointed toward the sky. "Geez, I can't see anything! I hope the creature can't see him." She did her best to keep her eyes on the sky, ready to fire at the creature if it came into view. "Wait, there it is!" She couldn't see the beast, but the red light glowing from its large eye could be seen easily as it flew above the fields. "It's going in the opposite direction. I think Grandpa's going to be OK." She sighed with relief. "Go, Grandpa, go!" she said quietly.

Joe made it to the creek and followed it down to the tree line. Either out of fear or pure adrenalin, he wasn't sure, but he didn't slow his pace until he reached the car. *That was too easy!* he thought. He stepped inside the car, started it, kept the headlights off like always, and made his way to the first house he and Mary had come across on their way to the farm.

Once Joe got about a half mile away, he turned on the headlights. As soon as the lights lit up the road in front of him, a figure came into view, standing in the middle of the road. He swerved the car away from it, nearly crashing into the ditch. Out of instinct, he slammed on the brakes and then looked back to see what he had almost hit.

"No, no, no! It can't be! That's Melinie!"

Standing in the road, now turned toward him, was his granddaughter. He could tell it was her by her face, but she was altogether something else. After catching his gaze, she began slowly walking toward the car. "Grandpa, where are you going?" Joe sat there, looking at her, wholly frozen from shock.

"Grandpa, I need your help!" she said as she picked up her pace.

Coming to his senses, he said, "Let her go!"

"What do you mean, Grandpa. It's me!" she said as she approached the car.

"You're not Melinie!" he yelled back.

Melinie let out a scream and began running toward the car. As she grew closer, her newly found wings lifted her into the air. "You can't leave! The master won't let you!" she shouted.

Then suddenly, she flew directly over the car, landing hard on top of the vehicle's hood, caving it in on the passenger side. Joe put the car into drive and stepped on the gas. As he sped off, he glanced back and forth between his side mirrors and his rearview mirror, but there was no sign of Melinie.

He must know what I'm doing! thought Joe. *I must get this done quickly and keep out of sight.* He again turned off the lights and pulled the car off to the side of the road. Before getting out, he looked in each direction to see if Melinie was still around; he didn't see her anywhere. "The house is less than a mile away. I'll walk from here and take the fields. Hopefully, the tall grass and camouflage will keep me hidden."

About thirty minutes later, Joe arrived at the first location he and his wife, Mary, had come across when they realized the house was no longer standing and the symbol had been removed. With the backpack in hand, he walked up the hill to the empty lot where the house once stood.

Where do I put this? he wondered. Looking around for something to mount the symbol, he found a wooden plank in the grass. Joe laid the board flat on the ground and applied the symbol made of clay on top of it. *How am I going to attach it?* he wondered. *I guess I'll just keep it here for now and then afterward find a way to make a permanent place for it.*

Joe pulled out the mason jar and poured about a third of the blood onto the symbol. The symbol didn't light up, meaning that at least one other symbol also needed to be replaced or required blood to be applied to it.

However, the symbol did something he didn't expect. It turned a bronze color like it had been hardened, then something that looked like tentacles grew from its sides and wrapped around the board, affixing it in place. "What is this?" Joe asked as he stumbled backward. A voice began whispering something he couldn't understand. The symbol slowly buried itself deep into the ground, and the whispering stopped.

"That's incredible!" Joe said. "The symbol must be making its permanent place. That's it! We must lay them on the ground so they can't be tampered with again. I must tell the others."

Joe grabbed the backpack, returned to the car, and took off to the next location. He figured that since he had placed the seal at the first site without confrontation with Melinie, she wasn't following him, and it was safe to take the car. When Joe arrived at the next house, the lights were on.

"Oh man, how am I going to do this? If Ben and Mable don't live here anymore, how will I get inside and check on the symbol?" Joe sat in his car for a few minutes, trying to figure out a game plan to get inside.

Tap, tap!

Joe nearly jumped out of his skin. Someone was tapping on his window. Staring at him through the glass was a middle-aged man he didn't recognize. "Are you Joe?" the man asked.

Joe rolled down the window. "Yes, I'm Joe. How do you know me?"

"My name is Brandon. My parents, Ben and Mable, told me about you and said you might show up one day. Are you here for the symbol?"

"Ah, yes, yes I am!"

"Please, come inside; I've been waiting for you. After what my boy saw last night, I am so glad you're here." The man's comments caught Joe off guard, but he took them as a sign. Joe got out of the car and followed Brandon into the house.

"I'm so glad you're here!" said Brandon. "My son Andrew was looking out the window last night and saw something that scared him."

"Is he OK?"

"He's shaken up, but I think he'll be OK."

"What did he see?"

"He saw a boy on a bike last night, and then a large monster with wings took him away."

Joe choked up for a minute, knowing the young boy must have seen Caleb.

"I thought he was just making it up until I walked outside this morning and found a bike with blood on the handlebars. I started to call the sheriff, and then I remembered the story my dad had told me about something he and others in the community saw many years ago. I called him, and he told me the creature may be back and that you would probably be coming to the house to check on the symbol on the wall downstairs."

"He told you about it?"

"Yes, when I was around twelve."

"Were you here when it happened all those years ago?"

"No, I was away at summer camp, thankfully!"

"Yes, that is good. What else?"

"Sorry to cut you off, but I'm guessing you need to get on this. Do you want to see the symbol?"

"Yes, please show me!"

Joe followed Brandon to the basement. "OK, it's here under the stairs behind the safe," Brandon said. He moved the safe away from the wall so Joe could view the symbol.

"Thank God! It's here!" Joe said.

"What does it do?" asked Brandon.

"It works with three others to bind the creature if the blood still covers it. Let me look; do you have a flashlight?"

Brandon handed Joe a flashlight so he could inspect the symbol.

"What is this?" Joe said.

"Sorry, my son told me that when we first moved in, he thought it would be cool to paint it. Is that a problem?"

"It would appear so!"

"What do we do?" Brandon said.

Joe reached into his bag and pulled out the other symbol and the mason jar filled with blood. "We use this one!"

Remembering what the other symbol had done on the dirt floor at the other site, Joe asked whether any part of the basement floor had dirt instead of concrete. "Yes! The partial crawl space at the other end has a dirt floor."

"Show me!"

Brandon took Joe to the crawl space section. "Here it is!"

"Perfect! Now, don't get scared by what you'll see!" Joe pulled out the symbol, placed it on the dirt floor in the crawl space, and poured the blood on it.

"No way!" Brandon yelled.

The symbol did the same thing it had done at the other site.

"How did it do that?" Brandon asked.

"I have no idea!"

"So, is it working?"

"If it were, it would light up, but it didn't," Joe said.

"What's that mean?"

"It means there is one more symbol I need to replace, and then we will be able to bind the creature again."

"Is there anything I can do to help?"

"Just keep your family safe and do not go outside until you hear from me."

"I can do that!"

"And one more thing," Joe said. "Can I use your truck?"

"The keys are on the kitchen counter."

"Thank you, Brandon!"

"Anything else?"

"If you're not a praying man, now might be a good time to start," Joe said with a smile.

"You know, you just might be right. Good luck, Joe!"

With that, Joe grabbed the keys to the truck, got inside, and headed to the last house on the list.

When Joe arrived at the last house, it was surrounded by fog. Hoping he wouldn't be noticed in Brandon's truck; he drove past the house. When he could no longer see the home from his rearview mirror, he turned off the lights before pulling off to the side of the road. "I guess I'll be walking from here."

Joe wasn't as familiar with this property as he was with the other ones, so finding a path without being seen would be tough. His only saving graces were the camouflage and his mascara-covered face, which didn't stay on as well as he had hoped. "I guess this wasn't the good stuff!" He chuckled.

He decided to walk on the road's shoulder until the house came into view and then to hit the woods. As he spotted the home, he noticed that someone or something was standing in the middle of the driveway. "Is that Melinie? It is!"

Melinie stood there with her wings outstretched, looking around as if she were keeping watch or looking for something.

Does she know I'm here?

He quickly received his answer to his question when Melinie called out, "I know you're out there, Grandpa! Did you think I didn't know you were in the truck? I have a surprise for you!"

Joe crouched down onto the road to keep out of her view.

"Here, let me show you!" Melinie briefly stepped into the fog out of Joe's view. "Come say hi!" Melinie stepped back into view. In each of her claws, she held something.

What are those? he wondered. "Can't see Joe? Here, let me walk a little closer," said Melinie.

Joe felt sick to his stomach. In one talon, she held a man; it was his son Mark. He looked completely limp. And in the other talon was a woman, his daughter-in-law, Amber. She was screaming.

"It doesn't have to be this way, Joe. Just come to me, and I will let them go!"

Joe didn't know what to do. He knew if he did what she said, this situation would never end. But he wasn't sure what would happen to Mark and Amber if he didn't yield.

"Aren't you their father, Joe? Don't you care about your family?"

Joe wanted so badly to do what she said to save them but knew he couldn't comply, and he just stayed still, watching in horror.

"Have it your way then!" Melinie drew Mark close to her face and dug her long fangs into his neck; she was draining his blood. Unable to save her husband, Amber kept screaming Mark's name.

"Stop, please!" Joe stood up and yelled.

"Well, hello, Grandpa!"

"Melinie, that's your parents! Why are you doing this?"

"Oh Joe, don't you know that I'm not Melinie anymore? And don't worry about Mark; he's not even here, and neither is Amber." Melinie stretched out her long arms to show him she wasn't holding anything.

"I saw them. Where are they?"

"I guess you aren't as smart as you thought. Let me help you. The fog is more than just fog. It is the essence of my master. It allows me to show you what I want you to see.

"I know what you're here to do, Joe. Aren't you tired of all of this? Don't you think you've put your family through enough? Do you think your grandkids are safe back at the farm? And my master just let you go, or was that just another illusion? How about that thing in your backpack? Is that real, or are you only seeing what we want you to see?"

Joe stood there, listening to Melinie. His mind raced at a hundred miles an hour. *Is she right? What do I do?*

"Joe, I'm getting impatient. Come to me now. It's time to end all of this!"

"You're right! I want this to end!" Joe walked toward Melinie with a look of defeat.

"That's right, Joe. You're making the right choice."

Joe approached Melinie with his hands behind his back.

"What are you hiding, Joe? What's in your hands?"

Joe continued walking toward Melinie, keeping his hands hidden from her.

"Joe, show me your hands now!"

Joe didn't respond and kept walking.

"Joe?" Melinie felt a burning sensation on her skin. "Joe, what do you have?"

When Joe first saw the fog around the house, he decided he would go ahead and prepare the symbol with the blood just in case he came face-to-face with Melinie or the creature. He wasn't sure if it would work, but they might also fear the symbol and blood since they feared the books.

Melinie hissed at Joe. "Stay away from me!" she screamed.

"Guess I'm smarter than you thought," he quipped.

"You will not win, Joe!"

"Maybe not, but I'm getting to that house!" Joe pulled out the blood-soaked symbol and ran toward Melinie.

Melinie screamed at Joe and flew toward him, knocking him to the ground. "It burns!" she cried. Joe quickly got to his feet and had a face-to-face standoff with her.

"You think you've won, Joe? This is only the beginning!"

Joe pointed the symbol toward Melinie and yelled, "Let her go!"

Melinie looked afraid for a moment and then laughed. "Tsk, tsk, Joe! Enjoy your little victory, but the war isn't over!" With that, she extended her wings and flew away.

Joe stood there momentarily to gather himself and make sure Melinie was gone before heading to the house. Seeing that he was alone, Joe then went to the house to do what he had come to do. "Time to end this!" Joe made his way into the vacant home.

He walked downstairs and didn't even look for the original symbol. After finding that this house also had a partial crawl space with a dirt floor, he placed the blood-soaked seal on the dirt floor. With a sigh of relief, he stood back as the symbol buried itself into the ground. Blinding him momentarily, a powerful beam of light filled the basement. "It worked! They're activated!" Joe shouted.

He had finished what he had sought to do. The symbols were activated, and soon the creature would be bound again. "It's over! It is done!" said Joe. He tried to stand up but fell from exhaustion. It became clear that his accomplishment was purely driven by adrenaline, and now his body was telling him it was time to rest.

"I guess I'll rest her for a while before heading back to the farm. I can't wait to see Mary again! I did it, sweetheart, I did it!" Joe said as he passed out from total exhaustion.

CHAPTER 11

TRANSFORMATION

Back at the farm, Joe's grandkids sat on the couch, talking to Brooke. "It's so good to meet all of you!" said Brooke. "All this time, I thought Dad was my only family. I knew there were blank spots in my mind, and I had to have other family members. Still, no matter what I tried, nothing worked to pull up any memories of them, and I was too scared to ask Dad questions about them because I couldn't get the vision of monsters out of my head every time I thought about it. I hope when all this is over, I can build a relationship with all of you!"

"Us too!" said Beth.

"Me too!" said Rachelle.

As they were talking, Rachelle saw something down the hall. "Beth, look!" said Rachelle. There was a bright light shining under the basement door.

"He did it!" said Brooke.

"The symbols are activated?" asked Beth.

"Yes, when they're activated, they light up," said Brooke. "Ouch, that burns!"

"What burns, Brooke?" asked Rachelle.

"The mark on my side. I don't remember that happening last time."

"Are you OK?" Beth asked.

"I think so, Beth! Wow, that really hurts!"

"So, what happens now?" asked Rachelle.

"Well, it's my turn now. I must stand in the middle of the books, and then …" Brooke began feeling the extreme weight of what would come next.

"Brooke, are you OK?" asked Beth.

"I'm scared! I know what I must do and that I was chosen for this, but I don't want to go through the torment again, and I don't want to forget all of you."

"I'm so sorry, Brooke. I wish there were another way. Maybe there is. Maybe …"

"There's no other way, Beth. I must do this."

Beth looked at Brooke. She could feel her pain and wished she knew what to say or had another option. "I don't know what to say, Brooke."

"It's OK, Beth. OK, ladies, I'm going to head to the basement. Please stay upstairs and close your eyes."

"Why do we need to close our eyes?" asked Rachelle.

"Do you want to see me turn into the thing you saw on the symbol?"

"I'm not scared!"

"Maybe not, Rachelle, but when I transform, the lights are blinding. My dad said he nearly went blind from it last time, and he wasn't even in the basement; he was looking down from atop the stairs. Please stay upstairs!"

"OK, we will," said Beth.

A loud crash occurred atop the house as Brooke approached the basement door. "Brooke, look out!" screamed Rachelle.

Brooke looked up in time to see the ceiling crashing down on top of her. "Brooke!" cried Beth. Beth and Rachelle watched as the ceiling collapsed on top of Brooke, completely covering her and filling the house with dust.

Coughing, Beth and Rachelle called out, "Brooke! Are you OK?"

Brooke didn't answer. Once the dust cleared enough for them to see, they ran to where Brooke had been standing when the ceiling came crashing down on her. "Brooke!" Beth called. "Are you OK?"

"Help! Get me out!" Brooke shouted. Beth and Rachelle worked quickly to remove the ceiling debris and get Brooke out.

"Rachelle, help me with this!" Beth was trying to move a large portion of the ceiling. Once Rachelle and Beth could move it to the side, they found Brooke. "Are you OK, Brooke?" asked Beth.

"I can't move my right leg; I think it might be broken."

"OK, we will get the rest of this off you and get you out!" said Beth.

After getting Brooke uncovered, it was clear that her leg was indeed broken; it was twisted to the side, and the shin bone was sticking out of the skin. "Oh, Brooke, that looks bad!" Rachelle said.

"Oh great! Help me to the couch, please!"

"I'm not sure we should move you!" said Beth.

"Um, look up!"

Beth looked up to see that a large tree was dangling in the hole in the ceiling. "Oh, my God!"

"Yeah, if that falls, I'm dead! You must get me away from here!"

Beth ran to the closest bedroom and returned with a large blanket. "OK, we will have to carry you in this."

"OK, just do it fast!"

Beth and Rachelle worked the blanket under Brooke, ensuring they did not touch her broken leg. Once it was completely under her, they grabbed two opposite corners on each side, lifted her, and carried her to the couch.

"We need to take care of this before you bleed out!" said Beth.

"I agree, but we can't call 9-1-1, and I assume neither of you has medical training."

"Unfortunately, no, we don't!"

"I am so cold!" Brooke said.

"You're going into shock! Rachelle, grab some more blankets so we can get her warm."

"OK!" Rachelle grabbed several blankets to help increase her body heat.

"Thank you, Rachelle!" said Brooke.

"Brooke, try to relax. Rachelle and I will get the first aid kit and do what we can to treat your wounds. Do your best to stay awake, OK? We don't need you passing out on us."

"I'll try! I need something for the pain, too; it hurts bad!"

Beth and Rachelle applied bandages to Brooke's leg but ensured they didn't cover the protruding bone. They then gave Brooke some painkillers they had found in the kitchen cabinet.

"OK, try to relax!" Beth said. "Rachelle and I will be back in a minute; we'll take a quick look at the ceiling."

"OK, be careful!"

"We will!"

"Beth, I thought we were safe in the house and that it couldn't attack us," Rachelle said.

"I'm guessing no one thought about the creature using something to damage the house. That tree is huge! If he can rip trees from the ground and throw them at the house, we are in real trouble!"

"Yeah, and with Brooke's broken leg, how will we get her downstairs? And if we find a way, will she still be injured if she transforms?"

"I don't know, sis."

"Should we wait for Grandpa before we even try to get her down there?" Rachelle said.

"In a normal situation, I would say yes, but is he coming back? We know he got the symbols placed, Rachelle, but what if he got caught afterward? We don't know. Either way, we must remove the debris from the basement door because it is completely blocked."

"Beth, that's risky! That tree could fall at any moment. I do not want to be underneath it when it does."

"So, what do we do then?"

"We wait."

"Wait for what?" Beth said.

"For either Grandpa to show up or for the tree to fall, whichever happens first."

"Yeah, that's what I'm saying! All right, we'll wait for now, Rachelle, but how long will those symbols stay activated? Is there a time limit? What if we miss the window?"

"I hear what you're saying, and who knows, but I still say we wait a bit longer; that tree might come crashing down any moment, you know?"

"I'll give it a half hour, and that's it, Rachelle!"

"Deal. A half hour." Beth and Rachelle returned to be with Brooke while waiting either for the tree to fall or for Joe to return.

After some needed rest, Joe abruptly woke up. *Oh, no, how long was I asleep? I must get back to the girls! They are probably scared out of their minds!* Joe thought. Feeling extremely confident that Brooke must have transformed by now and that the creature was undoubtedly bound again, Joe made his way without fear to Brandon's truck parked down the road.

Joe opened the door to the truck, tossed the backpack inside, and then ...

Whoosh!

He heard something fly over his head. "It can't be!" Joe tried to climb inside the truck, but Melinie grabbed him. He clung to the truck door with all his strength, but he wasn't stronger than Melinie; she pulled him into the sky.

"Melinie, let me go!" he shouted.

"Sorry, Grandpa! I told you the master would not let you get away!" Then everything went black as she covered his body with her wings and took him away.

"The half hour is up, Rachelle."

"Yeah, I know. Grandpa isn't back, and that tree is never going to fall."

"We need to make it come down or find another way downstairs!" said Beth. "The only other way is to climb through a downstairs window. That would mean going outside, and there's no way we can do that with her condition!"

"Well, then, we need to force the tree down!"

"How are we going to do that, Rachelle?"

"This place has an attic, right?"

"I suppose it does!"

"I'll climb into the attic and see if I can get over to it. If I can make it, then I'll try to kick it free."

"What if you fall?" Beth said.

"Dad and I used to climb trees together all the time; I think I can handle an attic!"

Beth didn't like the idea of sending Rachelle into the attic, but it was the only plan that might work. "OK, we can try it, but you be careful!"

"I always am! I'm not in the mood to die anytime soon. So that's my plan for getting the tree out. Do you have a plan for getting Brooke downstairs?"

"I'm working on it."

"Better hurry because, honestly, she's not looking good!"

"I know. I'm concerned for her," Beth said.

"Yeah, me too!"

"Let's find the attic access."

After locating the scuttle hole for the attic in the master bedroom closet, Rachelle grabbed a ladder from the utility room and scooted up it into the attic. "Hey, hand me a flashlight, Beth; it's dark up here!" After getting the flashlight from Beth, Rachelle made her way through the attic to where the tree was lodged inside the roof.

"I see it!" said Rachelle.

"Good. Can you work it free?"

"I must move a little closer first, but I think I can!"

As Rachelle moved closer to the tree, she felt the attic floor creak. "Whoa, this is bad!" She wrapped her arms around the roof joists in case the floor collapsed.

"How's it going, Rachelle?"

"Almost there! OK, I'm going to start kicking at it. Are you ready?"

"Yeah, go for it!"

Rachelle kicked at the tree once, but it didn't budge. She kicked a second time, and it looked like it had shifted some. "I think it's going to work! I will kick it as hard as I can several times to see if it will fall."

"OK, good luck!"

Rachelle kicked the tree a few more times, and it started to break free. As she went to kick it again, she heard a thump on the roof. "What was that?" She paused for a second but didn't hear anything. She kicked again, and—

Crash!

Something large hit the roof above her. Whatever it was, It didn't enter the attic, but she feared something else might come crashing down on her soon if she didn't hurry.

"Dang, I'm going to get trapped up here if the creature keeps throwing things at the roof!" Rachelle kicked the tree several more times before it broke free and fell hard on the hallway floor, filling the hallway with more dust.

Coughing from the dust, Beth said, "Way to go, sis! Now get out of there!" Rachelle made her way out of the attic just in time as another large tree crashed into the house, tearing through the roof and entering the attic, where she had been kicking to release the tree just moments ago.

"You did it!"

"Yep! Just in time too! Another tree hit the roof and landed right where I was sitting while trying to kick the tree free."

"Dang!"

"For sure! Now, how do we get her downstairs?"

"We use your mattress," Beth said. "It's just the right size to fit down the stairs. We lay her on it and strap her body down with ropes so she doesn't slide off."

"How about we use Dad's belts?"

"That's a great idea!"

"I know!" Rachelle responded with a chuckle.

"OK, I will go in front to keep it from sliding down too fast, and you will pull on it from the top to help lower it down slowly. Once we get her downstairs, we need to find a way to prop her up so she can stand in the middle of the books."

"Sounds like a good plan, Beth."

"I hope so; it's all I've got."

"Let's tell Brooke and get her ready."

"Brooke, we have a plan!" said Beth. After explaining the plan and getting Brooke's go-ahead, Rachelle retrieved her mattress from the bedroom, and Beth grabbed Mark's belts. They carefully laid Brooke on the mattress and strapped her down securely with their dad's belts. "Guys, I hope this works," said Brooke.

"I believe it will," said Beth. "But we need to hurry before we get hit by another tree."

"Yes, let's do this," said Brooke.

With Brooke securely strapped down on the mattress, Beth and Rachelle started pushing it toward the basement door. Just before reaching the door, Beth heard a knock on the front door. "Did you hear that?" Beth asked.

"Hear what?" asked Rachelle.

"I heard someone knocking on the front door."

"I didn't hear a knock," said Rachelle.

"I didn't hear anything either," said Brooke.

"I know I heard a knock."

"Leave it, Beth. We must get Brooke downstairs."

"OK!"

"Wait, there it is again! Someone *is* knocking. Give me a second; I need to check it out; it might be Grandpa."

"Beth! Don't!" Rachelle shouted.

"I'll be quick. I promise."

Beth walked slowly to the front door, and there was the knocking again. "Hello?" Beth asked.

"Beth, it's Grandpa. Hurry, let me in!"

"Grandpa?"

"Yes, it's getting closer; please let me in!"

Beth immediately opened the front door and saw her grandpa standing at the door. "You made it!"

"Yeah, just barely. The creature followed me, but I avoided getting caught."

Beth was so excited to see her grandpa that, without hesitation, she walked through the doorway and hugged him. "So happy you're here! We were getting ready to take Brooke downstairs so she could transform."

"That's great. Where is she?"

"She and Rachelle are in the hallway by the basement door."

"That's good. But they're not going to make it."

"What do you mean, Grandpa? Hey, you're holding me too tight! Grandpa, you're hurting my shoulders! Grandpa, let go; you're hurting me!"

Rachelle heard Beth talking to someone and walked over to the front door. "Beth, get away from it!"

Beth lifted her head from her grandpa's chest and saw that it was the creature, not her grandpa. "Let me go!" she shouted.

Rachelle grabbed the rifle leaning against the wall and pointed it at the beast. "Beth, move away!"

Beth tried to get away, but the creature's talons, which had dug deep into her shoulders, kept her from doing so.

"Beth, you have to move!"

"I can't!"

Rachelle had only one option. She had to wound her sister to get a shot off, or she would lose her too. "Beth, I'm so sorry!"

"No, Rachelle, don't!"

Rachelle fired a round from the rifle that grazed Beth's right shoulder but hit the creature in the chest. The impact separated the creature from Beth, knocking it off the front porch. Beth fell to the floor.

Rachelle put down the gun and ran to the front door to close it. After securing it with the deadbolt, she immediately checked on her sister. "Beth, are you OK? I'm so sorry! I didn't know what else to do."

"It's OK. You did the right thing."

"Can you stand?"

"With your help, probably."

Rachelle grabbed Beth's good shoulder and helped her to her feet. "Let me help you to the couch, and I'll get you bandaged up. I am so sorry!"

"It's OK. Luckily, you're a bad shot, and it just grazed my shoulder."

"Does it hurt?"

"Uh, yeah."

"Dumb question; I'm sorry."

Beth wanted to laugh, but it hurt too much.

"Yeah, that was a dumb question." Rachelle shrugged and laughed. "Well, one good thing came out of this, Beth."

"What's that?"

"My first aid skills have improved."

"Ouch! Don't make me laugh, Rachelle."

"Sorry, sis!"

"Hey, girls, was that a gunshot? Hey, what's going on?" Brooke yelled from across the room.

"Give me a minute! Everything is OK! I'll be right there!" After getting Beth bandaged up, Rachelle went over to Brooke. She explained what had just happened.

"Is Beth OK?"

"Yeah, apparently, Dad not teaching me to shoot yet wasn't a bad thing. The bullet barely touched her shoulder, but it did hit the creature; that's good, right?"

"Being shot isn't good, but yeah, that's better," Brooke said. "But like me, she will need a doctor soon, or she could get a major infection, even though it's a small wound."

"That's not good."

"No, not at all. The creature looked like my dad, Rachelle?" Brooke said.

"Yes, how can that be?"

"I have no idea! If it made her see my dad, it probably took him!"

"Oh, no!"

"We can't be sad right now, Rachelle! We need to focus on getting me downstairs!"

"How? Beth is injured, and you can't walk!"

"You're going to have to do it, Rachelle!"

"There's no way! I'm not strong enough by myself!"

"You must try; it's the only way!"

Rachelle knew Brooke was right, but how could she do it alone? "What if you fall off or the mattress slips down the steps too quickly? You could get even more injured."

"You can do this, Rachelle; I know it! Beth, tell her." Beth had managed to walk over to them.

"She's right, Rachelle! We're running out of time! You can do this!"

"OK, I will try!"

Rachelle positioned herself on the steps in front of the mattress. She placed her hands on the mattress and began pulling Brooke down the steps. "Are you sure, Brooke?"

"Yes, you can do this!"

Taking a huge breath, Rachelle braced herself and began pulling Brooke down the steps. "As you pull, I will grab each side of the steps to help keep it from going too fast!" Brooke said.

"OK!"

With Brooke holding onto the sides to help, Rachelle pulled the mattress downstairs one step at a time, stopping after each step to keep it from sliding down too fast and knocking her down. "Almost there. I can't believe it, Brooke!"

"You're doing great!"

"One more to go! It's going to drop off the last step hard, so be ready for it!"

"I'm ready!"

With one last pull, the mattress dropped to the basement floor. "Ouch, that hurt!" Brooke said.

"Sorry, Brooke!"

"It's all good! Rachelle, you did it!"

"I did! I'm stronger than I thought!"

"Proud of you!"

"Thanks! OK, now we must find something to prop you up on," Rachelle said. "Wow, those lights are blinding!"

"Don't stare at them. I'm not sure how they may affect your eyes."

Rachelle heard Brooke, but she found herself mesmerized by them. "I don't know what you're talking about. They don't bother my eyes at all. Where does the light come from?"

"We aren't sure. Rachelle, stop staring at the lights!"

"I will, I will, but they're so beautiful."

"Rachelle, what are you doing?"

"I want to touch them!"

"Beth, can you get down here? I need your help!"

Struggling to walk because of the intense pain from the gunshot, Beth made her way to the basement doorway. "What's going on?"

"I don't know. Rachelle is drawn to the lights, and I can't get her to listen to me. Can you make it down here?"

"I'll try." Beth grabbed the railing with her left arm and slowly descended the stairs. "Where is she? I can't see her."

"She walked over to the lights. It's too bright to see her, but I know she's over there."

"Rachelle, where are you?" Beth asked.

Rachelle didn't answer.

"Rachelle!"

Still no reply.

"Brooke, what's going on? Why is she drawn to the lights?"

"I'm not sure! Maybe, the blood bearer isn't supposed to be here when the books are activated. You must find her and get her away from them."

Beth moved toward the lights to find Rachelle. The intense light caused her eyes to burn. "Rachelle, where are you?"

Still no response.

"Brooke, my eyes feel like they are on fire!"

"Get out of there and help me get in the middle of the books."

"I have to get Rachelle out, though!" Beth said.

"You're going to burn your eyes out. Get out of there!"

Beth turned away from the lights and walked toward Brooke. "Brooke, I can barely see!"

"Follow my voice!"

Beth walked in the direction of Brooke's voice. The farther away she went from the lights, the better her vision became. "I am beginning to see better!"

"OK, keep walking!"

By the time Beth reached Brooke, the burning sensation was gone, and she could see normally again. "How did the light not bother Rachelle's eyes? I could barely handle it!"

"It must be related to her being the blood giver. We need to get over to the books right now! Beth, a large broom is leaning against the wall to my right. Get it and bring it to me. I can use it to walk. Keep your eyes shielded from the light."

"Got it!" Doing her best to keep her eyes away from the lights, Beth grabbed the broom and brought it to Brooke.

"OK, now hand it to me."

Beth handed the broom to Brooke. "Now, here's the hard part, Beth. I'm going to need you to help me up!"

"This is going to be fun!"

"Oh, so fun!" Brooke said.

With the broom in one hand and Beth holding Brooke's other hand, Brooke managed to get to her feet. "Just keep me from falling as I hop on one leg."

"Won't the lights burn your eyes too?"

"Nope! I guess that comes with the job description. Here's the other fun part. You must keep your eyes closed as you help me to the books."

"Oh, great!"

"Yeah, I lied about it being the fun part!"

"Uh-huh!"

"Ready?"

"No, but let's do it anyway!"

"All righty!"

With Beth's help, Brooke hopped on one leg toward the lights. "Move to the right a little, Beth, so we can head directly toward the middle."

"Is this better?"

"Perfect! We are halfway there."

"What happens if we can't get Rachelle out before you transform?" Beth said.

"I'm not sure. Hopefully, she will be OK, but I can't say, Beth."

While helping Brooke walk, Beth yelled, "Rachelle, where are you?"

"I'm right here!" Suddenly, Rachelle appeared right in front of them.

"Rachelle, are you OK?" asked Beth.

"I'm great! Isn't it beautiful, Beth?"

"Brooke, is Rachelle OK?" Beth said. "Can I open my eyes?"

Rachelle's eyes were solid white. "Something is wrong with her, Beth; I think she's blind. I don't see her pupils."

"My eyes are fine, Brooke. I can see things better than ever. Open your eyes, Beth, and see for yourself. You need to see what I see."

"Beth, don't open your eyes! Don't look at the light!" said Brooke.

"Rachelle, what do you see?" asked Beth.

"I see how things are. We were wrong about everything. The creature is not here to hurt us but to save us. Open your eyes, Beth!"

"Beth, don't listen to her! I don't know what she sees, but what she says is untrue. We know the fog changes our perception of reality, and the lights must do it too. We need to go around her and get this done."

"Rachelle, please come out of the lights and let us pass by," Beth said. "What you're seeing is a trick. Please move away!"

"I'm sorry, Beth, but I can't. It would be best if you saw it for yourself. Here, let me help you."

Rachelle pulled Beth away from Brooke and forced her eyes open. Brooke lost her balance and fell to the floor without Beth's support. When she fell, she landed on her broken leg, causing her to scream in pain.

Brooke lay on the floor, calling, "Beth, close your eyes! Beth, can you hear me?"

"Brooke, help!" Beth cried.

Brooke did her best to stand up independently but kept falling back onto the floor. Each time she fell, her leg pain grew worse. *I must get to her!* "Beth, I'm coming! Keep your eyes shut. Beth, can you hear me?"

Brooke knew that if she didn't act quickly, Beth would eventually open her eyes too. She thought about crawling, but there was no way she could lie on her stomach and crawl with a broken leg. *Maybe I can scoot myself that way*, she thought.

Brooke moved to a sitting position, turned her body around with her back facing the lights, and began pushing off the floor while keeping her legs straight. "It's working! Beth, I'm coming. Keep your eyes shut; I'm almost there!" As she continued to scoot toward the lights, she hit something with her back that caused her to stop. She looked around to see what it was. "Beth?"

"Hi, Brooke!" Beth said.

"Are you OK, Beth?" She couldn't see her very well with her body facing away from Beth. "Are you OK?"

"I'm more than OK, Brooke! Aren't the lights beautiful?"

Brooke felt shivers run up her spine. "No, Beth, no!"

"It's OK, Brooke! Rachelle was right!" Beth walked around to the front of Brooke and knelt in front of her. Her eyes were just like Rachelle's, all white with no pupils.

"We don't have to worry anymore," Beth said. "The creature is here to save us from all the pain we've had. I finally understand why he's here. He can even heal your injuries, Brooke. My shoulder injury is gone; let him do the same for you. We need to join him so we can be free."

"That's right, Brooke, listen to Beth," Rachelle said. "The master is here to save us all from our pain!" She made her way next to Beth on the floor.

"No, no, he's lying to you, girls," Brooke said. "He's not here to save us. Listen to me! Help me to the books so we can stop this."

Beth and Rachelle stood up. "You should've listened to us, Brooke!" said Rachelle. "He had a plan for you, but if you will not listen to the truth, he has no choice but to—"

"Hello?" a female voice called from atop the basement stairs. "Hello? Is anybody down there?"

"Help me!" Brooke called out. Immediately, she heard someone running down the stairs.

"Where are you?" the person called.

"Over here!" Brooke said.

"I can't see you; it's too bright!"

"Don't look at the lights; it's not safe!"

"OK! How do I get to you?"

"Shield your eyes, look down at the floor, and follow my voice."

"OK, I'm coming your way. Oh my God, Brooke! Are you OK!" A woman with a somewhat familiar face stared down at Brooke. She knelt on the floor before Brooke, still shielding her eyes. "Brooke, what happened?"

Brooke sat silently for a moment, trying to process who this woman was and why she was at the farm. "Do I know you?" asked Brooke.

"You do, but you don't remember me. I'm your younger sister, Valerie."

"My sister?"

"Yes!"

"Were you one of the monsters I saw as a kid?"

Valerie's eyes filled with tears, and she said, "Yes, I was one of those! I'm so sorry, sis. We tried to make you see, but ..."

"It's OK; it wasn't your fault. We can discuss it later, but I need your help now! The lights have pulled in Beth and Rachelle, and now they are under the creature's control."

"Where?" Valerie started to look around.

Brooke grabbed Valerie's face and said, "No, don't look! If you look at them, you'll be under its control too!"

Valerie turned away from the lights and fixed her gaze on Brooke. "Where are they, Brooke?"

"They were right here! I guess they went back inside when they heard you."

"How can I help?"

"I need to get to the books in the middle of the lights. Can you help me get up?"

"I will try!"

"I need that broom to brace myself on, and then I'll need you to support me as we walk. Can you do that?"

"I think so!"

With Valerie's help, Brooke once again got to her feet. "As we walk, I need you to keep your eyes closed. I will guide you, but no matter what, don't open your eyes, OK?"

"OK!"

"Once we reach the middle, I will hop inside to transform and finish this. Once I'm inside, run upstairs and stay there until it's done."

"OK, Brooke!" With her eyes closed, Valerie helped Brooke as they moved toward the lights.

"Keep moving; we're almost there, Valerie!"

"Aunt Valerie?"

Valerie heard her name being called from somewhere in the basement. "Beth? Rachelle? Is that you, girls?"

"Valerie, don't listen to them! They are trying to stop you."

"Aunt Valerie, don't listen to Brooke," Rachelle said. "Her eyes are closed to the truth. Don't you remember the heartache and pain you experienced from losing your sister for all those years? Do you want to go through that again? Just open your eyes so you can see the truth. You were told a lie. He's not here to hurt you or anyone else but to save us from our pain. Just look, and you will see!"

"Valerie, don't look!" Brooke cried. "Please, don't look!"

"Don't worry, sis; I'm not stupid enough to believe what they say. Dad told me everything years ago. Now, keep hopping, and let's get this over with."

"We're in the lights, and I can see the books, Valerie!" Brooke said.

"My eyes are burning, sis!"

"Keep them shut!"

"They are, but they're still burning!"

"Just a few more feet; hang in there!"

"I'm trying! Something's got me, Brooke!"

Beth and Rachelle grabbed Valerie by the shoulders and began pulling her backward. "Stop pulling, sis," Brooke said. "I'm going to fall!"

"Beth and Rachelle are pulling me backward! You must hop over there now!"

"Stop!" Beth shouted. "The master cannot be bound again!"

Rachelle and Beth continued pulling Valerie away to keep Brooke from reaching the books. With one hard pull, Valerie was forced to let go of Brooke. Brooke hit the floor backward, hitting her head on the concrete floor. She could barely move between the intense pain in her leg and the impact of her head hitting the floor.

"Brooke, do it now!" screamed Valerie.

Brooke was in so much pain that she struggled even to stay conscious. "I have to get up!" she said to herself. She tried to sit up, but the room kept spinning, making it impossible to focus.

"Brooke, wait! Beth and Rachelle were telling the truth," Valerie said. "I see now! We can't bind him. If we do, we are lost forever."

"No, not you too, Valerie!"

"No, it's OK, sis! I see the truth now. I have a gift for you. I have been given the power to heal. As I said, he's here to take our pain away. Wait for me, and I'll show you. He wants me to heal your injury to prove that he's good. Wait right there; I'm coming to you."

Brooke wasn't going to wait for Valerie. She knew she had to find a way to get to the books no matter how much pain she was in. *This is going to hurt!* With one quick motion, Brooke spun her body over until her stomach was on the floor. She screamed in agony. *Fight through it!* she told herself. Then she began pulling herself toward the books with only her hands and arm strength. *Almost there!*

"Brooke, no, stop!" Valerie said. "Let me heal you! Stop!"

Brooke kept going until her body was in the center of the books. She flipped onto her back, grabbed her knees with her arms, and quickly drew her legs to her chest; the pain was debilitating. "I made it!"

Immediately, the lights faded, and the room grew pitch black. "What's happening? It's different this time!" Brooke said. When she was younger, the lights had turned brighter right before she transformed. This time, everything was dark, and she could hear strange sounds from inside the darkness. It sounded like people screaming in pain.

She tried to cover her ears, but this didn't help to muffle the sounds; the screams became deafening. "Stop!" she shouted, but they didn't stop. She lifted herself onto her knees; her leg was healed. *The pain is gone!*

Suddenly, faces appeared from the darkness; they were all around her; these were the people she had heard screaming.

"Stop! Please stop!" she cried. Brooke wondered if she was losing her mind. "Is this real? Am I here? Is my leg really healed? What is happening?"

More and more faces revealed themselves, and with them came more and more screaming.

"Don't be afraid!" a voice said. Suddenly, the screaming stopped. "I had to get your attention! I had to make you see!"

Brooke took her hands off her ears and made eye contact with the entity speaking with her. It didn't look at all like the creature they'd been fighting. It looked human, but just like the other creature, it had large wings. Its eyes were filled with fire, and it held a large golden sword. "Who are *you*? Who were those people, and why were they screaming?"

"My name cannot be spoken with the human tongue. Who I am is beyond your comprehension. Those you saw screaming in the darkness are the tormented souls I've come to set free. Do not be afraid, my child. I appear before you now because you have been chosen."

"Chosen? Chosen for what? I-I-I don't understand!"

The entity reached out his hand to Brooke and said, "Come with me!"

Brooke grabbed the entity's hand, not understanding why she would do such a thing. After doing so, she suddenly found herself in a dimly lit cave.

"Where am I?" she said.

"I have taken you to where it all began. Long ago, I ruled as a king over the stars. I was more beautiful than any other creature, and all that was made worshipped me. When mankind breathed its first breath, I was there to witness it. I was there to give them knowledge and understanding. I was there to guide them and teach them the forbidden truths. However, there was one who didn't appreciate me for offering my gifts to mankind. That entity chained me to this cave for thousands of years. Day and night, I cried out to be free. Then one night, a young man heard my cries. He also felt chained and unappreciated by those over him. Over time, he accepted my gifts and chose to be like me. This is the one whom you feel compelled to bind to the earth."

"You are the one who transformed him?"

"Yes! He just wanted to be free! He just wanted to be like me. It's not what you've been told. I want to give freedom to mankind. To provide them with what they truly desire—not be stripped of their understanding but to be free and powerful. You believe you were called to be the one who binds my servant back to the cave, but you were deceived by the same one who bound me. He tricked you into giving up your family and your freedom to be forever tormented. I am the truth; he is a liar. Come with me, Brooke, and I will make you a queen. You will join me at my side and rule how you were intended to from the beginning; this is what you've been chosen for."

Brooke was taken aback by what the entity had said. *Was I wrong this whole time?* "Wait, if you're so benevolent and he's so good, why did he take my family and others? Why did he try to hurt us?"

"My dear, it was all for preservation. Wouldn't you fight back if someone tried to chain you up? He wasn't given a chance."

"Well, what about my niece Melinie? He possessed her body. Is she like him now?"

"Yes, she is, but that was her choice. She was tired of being afraid. She was tired of being a victim, and now she's like a god. You can all be like gods."

"I don't want to be a god. I want all of this to stop!"

"It can, Brooke, it can! I can make it all stop right now. It's your choice."

"How is it my choice? How do I make it stop?"

"Just step away from the books before the transformation begins."

"I'm still in the middle of them?"

"Yes! You're not really in the cave. I have used my essence to show you all this, but you must choose quickly. The darkness gave me a short time to talk with you. Once it fades, your transformation will start, and then it will be too late."

"Show me the basement!"

"Brooke, the darkness is fading; make the choice now!"

"Get out of my head!"

"Brooke, it's almost time; step away from the books!"

"Leave me alone!"

"I can set you free, Brooke. Grab my hand, and you will be reborn!"

"No!" Brooke shouted.

"Have it your way, Brooke!"

The entity disappeared into darkness, and Brooke found herself back in the basement.

"Brooke, get away from the books!" screamed Valerie.

Brooke looked around her; she could see that the darkness was beginning to fade, and the light from the books was getting brighter. The faces surrounding her were nearly gone, and the screams were quiet. "It's starting!"

Brooke felt her body being lifted into the air. Four massive golden wings extended out from her shoulder blades, two extending upward and two extending downward. Her hands and feet became elongated with sharp, eagle-like talons protruding from them, and her eyes became like fire. She let out a loud, warlike scream that shook the entire house, then flew straight up through the roof and into the sky.

Her scream and ascension into the sky knocked Valerie, Beth, and Rachelle off their feet. "What happened?" asked Beth.

Valerie ran over to her and said, "She's transformed! We're no longer under his power!"

Rachelle ran upstairs to see for herself. "Come up here!"

Valerie and Beth ran upstairs and onto the front porch. "Look, she's flying!" said Rachelle.

"What's she holding onto?"

"It's the cage. Just like the one on the symbol," said Valerie. All three stood there, watching this incredible event that had just happened.

"I can't believe what I'm seeing!" said Beth.

"I know! It's almost over, girls!" said Valerie.

Like lightning, Brooke streaked across the night sky. Just moments later, they heard an awful scream far into the woods. "Is that the creature?" Rachelle asked.

"I think so! My dad said it took much fighting last time to bind him. I don't think he will give up any quicker this time."

"Hey, who are they?" asked Rachelle.

A group of people stood in a line facing the farm just a short distance from the house. "I don't know!" said Valerie.

"Wait, who's that?" asked Beth. "Is that Melinie?"

Melinie stood in the middle of the group. She towered high above the other people standing with her. "What is she doing?" asked Rachelle.

"I think she is leading them," said Valerie.

"Leading them where?"

"Here!" said Beth. "I think she's leading them here."

"What do you think of me now, Beth?" shouted Melinie.

"Melinie, what are you doing?" Beth shouted back.

"Isn't it obvious? I've accepted the truth of who I am supposed to be. Unlike you, I took the offer of a new life; I have been reborn and have become a god!"

"You're not a god, but you are my sister, and I love you!" Beth said. "Don't do this, Melinie! Come back to us, and we will find a way to help you!"

Melinie laughed at Beth. "I don't need your help! You need mine. I will give you one chance to surrender so you can become as I am."

"I can't, sis!"

"Then you are no longer my sister!"

Melinie spread her wings and flew high above the people under her control. "Go and bring them to me!" she shouted. "They are rejected; they are the enemy of our master!"

The group of mind-controlled people began marching toward the farm.

"They're coming! Close the door and get back to the basement!" Valerie shouted. Valerie and her two nieces ran to the basement for a place to hide. Within seconds, trees and other large objects began hitting the house.

"Melinie is going to make the house fall on us!" Rachelle shouted.

A large tree crashed through the home, collapsing the main floor and landing in the basement. "Get under the stairs!" Valerie shouted.

The three of them huddled under the stairs, hoping to evade the onslaught of objects being hurled at the house. "Will Brooke fight Melinie and the other people, too?" asked Rachelle.

"I don't know! There's so many of them!" said Beth.

"Can they get inside?" asked Rachelle.

"I hope not!" said Valerie.

While they continued hiding in the basement, Brooke hunted for the creature. She found him hiding deep in the woods. After dropping the cage at the cave entrance, which had now become visible, she flew through the trees and stabbed him in the chest with razor-sharp talons. Keeping her claws deep inside his chest, she carried him to the cage and forced him inside. The creature was severely wounded but wasn't ready to go down without a fight. When she went to close the door, he slashed her abdomen with his claws and stabbed her in the eye with a knifelike tail, but the wounds in her stomach and eye healed immediately.

The creature flew into the air to escape from her, but she was too quick. The fire in her eyes burned his wings, causing the beast to fall hard onto the ground. "You cannot win!" he hissed.

"Be silent!" Brooke demanded. "You are bound once more!" She threw the creature into the cage and sealed it shut with blood she had drawn from her hand. "In this cell, you will remain. With blood, you shall be bound!"

Then Brooke took a book out from under her wings. With words no one could understand, she recited what was in the book. Once done, the cave entrance opened, and she pushed the cage inside. Using the book again, she spoke more words from within its pages, and the cave walls closed over the creature and the cage holding him captive. The cave then disappeared.

"It is complete!" she said.

Slowly, Brooke began to return to her former self. Her wings retracted back inside her shoulders. Her arms and legs returned to normal. Her eyes were no longer filled with fire. After the transformation was complete, Brooke collapsed in the field.

Back at the farm, everything suddenly went quiet. No more objects or trees were being thrown against the house. "Is it over?" Rachelle asked.

"Let's go see!" said Beth.

"Wait. Before we go upstairs, let's look out the basement window," said Valerie. Valerie walked to one of the basement windows to look outside. The group of people was no longer marching toward the house. Their eyes looked normal, and they were talking to one another. "I think it's over!" said Valerie.

Excitedly, they ran upstairs and out the front door to see everyone.

"Dad!" screamed Rachelle.

"Mom!" cried Beth.

"Girls!" The girls ran to Mark and Amber, giving them the biggest hugs ever.

"You guys are OK!" said Beth.

"Looks like it! What happened?"

"That is a very long story."

"Girls, what happened to the house?" asked Mark with huge eyes.

"Well, Dad, we have a lot to tell you," Beth said as she looked at Rachelle and giggled a little.

"Daddy! Mommy!"

Mark and Amber turned around to see little Chase running toward them. Mark knelt with his arms stretched out, and Chase jumped into them. "I missed you so much, little buddy! Are you OK?"

"I'm OK, but I had a really weird dream."

"We all did; we all had weird dreams, buddy."

Amber kissed his cheek and said, "We will never leave again. I love you so much, Chase."

"I love you too, Mommy."

When Beth saw Chase with their mom, she nearly collapsed. She was afraid she had lost him forever, and now that he was back, she found it hard to control her emotions. "Chase, come here!" she told him. Chase ran over to Beth, and she scooped him up in her arms.

"Why are you crying, sissy? Are you hurt?"

"No, I'm not hurt. I just missed you so much!"

"Why?"

"I thought I lost you!"

"You didn't lose me; I'm right here."

"Yes, you are, and I'm never letting you go again."

"OK. Can we play?"

"Of course, we can! Tag, you're hit!" Chase giggled, and Beth chased after him.

"Hey, where's my hug?" said a voice.

Mark, Amber, and their girls turned to see Caleb walking up the field.

"Caleb!" Beth ran to him and embraced him. "I was so scared for you! I'm so glad to see you!"

"Great to see you too, sis!"

"What happened to you?"

"Melinie happened to me! You should have seen her; she is different now. She turned into one of those things and took me. Is she back too?"

"I haven't seen her yet!" Beth said. "I hope so! Let's go ask Dad."

"Jay!" shouted Mark.

"Hey, Mark!"

"Good to see you, man!"

"Good to be seen!"

"How are you feeling?"

"Like I've been hit by a train."

"Yeah, I know the feeling."

"Do you know what happened, Mark?" Jay said.

"I do. I will explain it all to you, buddy; I promise."

"OK! And Mark?"

"Yeah?"

"Next time you need a favor, don't ask me."

"Got it, buddy," Mark said with a laugh. "Valerie, where is Brooke?"

"I'm not sure, Mark! She went after the creature, and we haven't seen her."

"Let's go find her! Everyone, we need to find Brooke! Come with me!"

"Hey. Wait for me!" said Joe.

"Grandpa, you're here!" said Beth.

"Yes, sweetheart, it looks like we're all here. Brooke did it, didn't she?"

"Yes, she did. I guess it's all over."

"Wait, Grandpa, have you seen Melinie? I don't see her here with us."

"Maybe she's with Brooke. We will find her. Don't worry."

With everyone scouring the woods, Beth found Brooke lying in the tall grass several yards away from the house. "I found her!"

Everyone came running to see.

"Brooke, sweetheart, are you OK? It's Dad!"

Brooke slowly opened her eyes. "Dad?"

"Yes, it's me!"

"Mom?"

Mary looked at Brooke. "You remember me?"

"Of course, Mom!"

Crying with joy, Mary ran to Brooke and embraced her. "My girl is back! Thank you, God! I missed you so much!"

"I missed you too, Mom!"

"It worked, Dad!" said Brooke.

"Yes, Brooke, it worked. You did it!"

"I'm so glad, Dad, but if he's bound, why do I remember everyone!"

"I don't know; luck, grace, or something else … either way, we must be happy that it's finally over, and we *all* have you back!"

Brooke smiled and gave Joe another big hug.

"Grandpa?"

"Yes, Beth?"

"Melinie is still missing!"

"Everyone, my granddaughter Melinie is missing!" Joe said. "Please help me find her!"

"Grandpa, the last time we saw her, she was in the field. She was leading everyone to the house," said Beth.

"Has anyone seen my granddaughter Melinie? She was in the field with all of us," Joe said to the group. No one could remember seeing Melinie.

"Dad, we have to find her!" said Mark.

"We *will* find her, Mark!" said Joe. "We will not give up until we do!"

"Dad, what was that sound?" asked Valerie.

"What did it sound like?"

"Like something flew over us. Do you think …"

"No, it wouldn't be the creature!" said Brooke. "I remember putting him in the cage and closing it over him. He's bound!"

"You remember doing that?" asked Joe.

"Yeah, I do; it's all different this time, Dad," said Brooke.

"OK, well, maybe it was an actual bird," said Valerie.

"That would be nice," Joe said. "Now, let's get back to searching for Melinie; she has to be here on the farm somewhere."

"Valerie?" a voice said.

"Dad, did you hear that?"

"Hear what?"

"Someone said my name."

"I didn't hear anything. Did someone say Valerie's name?"

Everyone denied calling her name.

"I think I'm losing it, Dad," Valerie said.

"It's OK; we are all stressed and exhausted. Why don't you head to the house and rest up? We will keep searching for Melinie."

"Are you sure, Dad?"

"Yeah."

"OK, but let me know the moment you find her."

"OK, sweetheart."

As Valerie turned toward the house, Melinie dropped from the sky and stood before her. "Dad! Help!"

Hearing Valerie scream for help, Joe saw Melinie standing before his daughter. "Melinie, what are you doing? We were looking for you!" yelled Joe.

"Were you, Grandpa? Well, here I am. How do you like the new me?"

"I like you just fine, Melinie. You're my granddaughter."

"Don't lie to me, Joe! You are just like everyone else. You have rejected me, and I can see now that you even fear me."

"I don't fear you, sweetheart; I love you. Let us help you."

"Help me what? Help me to be like all of you? Fragile? I don't think so!"

"Your master is bound; why didn't you change back?"

"Oh, Joe, didn't I say you might have won the battle, but I would win the war? Your precious little books aren't powerful enough to bind more than one of us at a time, and my master knew that. That's why he took me when he did. He needed me to transform before Brooke became the key. Now I am the ruler of the night, and one day I will free my master by speaking his name."

"I will not tell you his name!"

"Not willingly, Joe, but you will tell me."

"Why would I do that?"

"You will have no choice!"

With Joe and the other family watching, Melinie placed her hands on Valerie's shoulders. Her long talons dug deep into Valerie's flesh. "Dad!" Valerie screamed in pain.

"Please let her go!" shouted Joe.

"Tell me his name!" Melinie said.

"I can't!"

"So be it!"

"Melinie, please don't take her!" Joe said.

"Who is this Melinie? I am she who is unseen, she whose name is unwritten."

With an evil smirk, Melinie wrapped her wings around Valerie and ascended into the sky. "You will tell me his name, Joe! Oh, and before I leave, I have something for *you*, Beth."

"Melinie, please don't do this!" said Beth.

"I left something for you in the woods behind the house. Consider it a farewell gift. I will see you again, Joe. Soon my transformation will be complete, and none of you will be hidden from me. Even now, I can feel my master's eye forming inside my chest." Then just like that, Joe and his family watched in horror as Valerie was taken from them.

As Joe helplessly watched his daughter being taken, he started to run after her when Brooke touched his shoulder and said, "Dad, I feel strange."

Joe grabbed his daughter as she collapsed to the ground. "What's wrong, Brooke?"

"I feel dizzy, and my side is on fire." Brooke lifted her shirt to show Joe her side.

"Oh, no!" Joe said.

"What is it, Dad?"

"The mark is gone, Brooke!"

"How?"

"I'm not sure."

"If it's gone, how are we going stop Melinie?"

"We can't." Holding Brooke in his arms, he kept looking into the sky for Valcric, wondering if he'd ever see her again. *I can't lose her. Will I be forced to tell Melinie his name?* These were his silent thoughts, and no one could know; for the sake of his daughter, he had to make a decision.

Beth felt a sickening feeling. What had Melinie left in the woods for her? "Dad, I need to see what Melinie was talking about."

"She was probably trying to get under your skin. Don't waste your time."

"Dad, I haven't seen Zack."

"I'll go. You stay here."

"OK, Dad."

Mark walked to the woods behind the house. He was afraid of what he might find. A few minutes later, Mark returned to his family.

"Dad, did you find anything?" Beth asked.

Mark looked at his daughter with tears in his eyes.

"Dad?"

Mark shook his head. "I'm so sorry, Beth!"

Beth knew her dad had found Zack in the woods and that he wouldn't be coming back. She collapsed to the ground. "Why would Melinie do this?" she cried.

"It wasn't Melinie. My little girl wouldn't—she couldn't do such a thing," Mark said, weeping in disbelief.

Mark had found Zack's body nailed to a tree with a sharpened tree branch. His neck had been broken, and it had bite marks like something had fed on him. Melinie had used her claws on his chest to scratch the words "Tell me his name!"

Joe and his family had thought the nightmare was over, but it had only begun. Besides Joe, they didn't know the name of the creature they had just bound in the cave, but now the "unseen and unwritten" creature had a name they knew well and loved; she was a daughter, granddaughter, and sister; her name was Melinie.

Without the key, how will they stop Melinie? Can she be turned back? What will happen if Joe tells Melinie the creature's true name? Will Melinie give Valerie back or release the creature from his prison and release something even more evil on the community? These are the questions yet to be answered.

ABOUT THE AUTHOR

J. A. Robinson has been using his active imagination to write stories for decades. This tale is a darker version of the story he told his five children and is dedicated to them. *Lemoy and His Dark Return* is his first novel.

Printed in the United States
by Baker & Taylor Publisher Services